ALPHA'S MOON

RENEE ROSE

LEE SAVINO

Published in the United States of America

Midnight Romance, LLC

WANT FREE BOOKS?

Go to http://subscribepage.com/alphastemp to sign up for Renee Rose's newsletter and receive a free books. In addition to the free stories, you will also get special pricing, exclusive previews and news of new releases.

Download a free Lee Savino book from www.leesavino.com

CHAPTER 1

PUERTO RICO

eke

The Puerto Rican jungle is thick and humid. At night, the song of the *coquí* frogs chorus echo all around the stifling darkness. I creep silently over the rotting leaves on the rain-forest floor, slinking into position. Channing's already there on his belly, squinting through the sight of his sniper rifle.

"We got two guards on deck," Channing whispers.

With our shifter hearing, we don't need comms units to hear each other. Nor do I need night vision goggles. That's the reason Colonel Johnson created a special ops team composed entirely of shifters. He's one of us. He knew how much we'd be capable of when our abilities didn't have to be hidden from our human counterparts.

A quick glance, and I clearly see the outline of two cartel members standing in front of the shack's open door frame. Each of them hold machine guns.

"What do you think—hostage inside?" Channing murmurs. "Tied, gagged?"

"Gagged. Tied with rope." That's my guess, anyway.

"Don't see any dogs," Channing says. "So we wait for Rafe's signal."

I nod and strip out of my outer clothes, including dog tags. Colonel Johnson had special camo underclothing designed for us. The fabric is stretchy and flexible enough to accommodate both human and wolf form. I guess the army higher ups thought having our ding-dongs hanging out after we shifted back would make us feel vulnerable. Like we give a shit who sees us naked.

I shift, but try to maintain some control, to hold back my wolf. He's antsy to get on with the hunt. The sad truth is that after years of war conditioning, he's always ready for the kill, especially when there's a civilian rescue involved. The need to protect sometimes overwhelms reason.

The signal is a long blast on a dog whistle, a sound no human can hear. When it comes, Channing and I dart forward. As a wolf, I'm faster, and I race ahead.

We're almost there when I pick up a rumbling sound up the road. Trouble coming in the form of an old diesel truck. Fuck! More kidnappers showing up to help stand guard.

My ears prick at the ear splitting sound of the dog whistle. Two short blasts this time—Rafe telling us to get out.

I try to turn back. To follow orders. The part of me that still knows chain of command fights for control.

But my wolf isn't having it.

It's too late—I smell the package. The frightened human who's perhaps given up on being rescued.

It's wrong to disobey a command. We may not be Special Ops any more, but wolves also follow their leader, and Rafe is our alpha. Still, I can't stop my wolf. He needs to save the human. I bound forward, paws eating up ground as I head toward the shack.

"Abort mission," Channing growls, but I'm too far gone. I leap, a silent shadow, onto the wooden platform.

The first guard dies almost silently. His body thumps to the deck. The other guard whirls, fingers scrambling for the trigger of his machine gun when two hundred plus pounds of wolf lands on him. He goes down, and I silence him with my teeth.

Permanently.

I hear shots and raise my head. My muzzle is slick, and there's blood in my mouth. On the other side of the shack, our team attacks the diesel truck. I forced them into this by not following orders. It's the only option now.

A few more shots, a growl from Lance's wolf, and the sound of screams drowns out the chorus of *coquí* frogs for a moment. Then the truck engine cuts off, and there's silence.

"Goddammit, Deke!" Channing whisper-shouts. He's still in human form, slinking up to the deck with his rifle outstretched. "You were supposed to follow orders."

My wolf bares his teeth at him.

"Fucking *loco*," Channing mutters as he brushes by me. He follows proper protocol, casing each dark corner before entering the shack. A few seconds later, he starts talking in a low, soothing voice to the hostage.

I'm glad he can because I would scare the hell out of her.

I growl and turn away, my nose to the ground, making sure all threats have been eliminated.

Gangsters: dead. Hostage: rescued. Mission accomplished. The only problem? The action was over in less than ninety seconds. My wolf wants more.

I lope off the deck and around the shack to the diesel truck. There's blood spattered on the cab and two gang members dead—one in the front seat, one a few feet from the passenger door.

Lance stands nearby, disassembling the target's semi-automatics. He's in his camo underclothing from shifting. His dog tags glint on his bare chest—he didn't have time to remove them before shifting.

"Fuck, Deke," he greets me. "I ruined a good pair of khakis for you." He wrenches the metal gun pieces apart and drops them into an open bag at his feet.

I make myself useful, loping back up the hill to Lance's stakeout spot to retrieve his pack. We keep an extra change of clothes for this contingency. Lance hadn't expected to shift, but to finish the mission, my wolf's defiance forced him to. My pack brothers always have my back no matter what.

"Thanks," Lance grunts when I return. He dresses quickly.

"Let's move out. Channing's already gone with the package." The *package* being the hostage. The one we, as mercenaries, were just paid a sizable amount of money to retrieve for someone high up in our government who didn't want to risk an active military team on this job. "Rendezvous at HQ."

A crackle in the brush behind me announces the arrival of my alpha.

"What the hell was that, soldier?" Rafe growls at me even though we're no longer technically soldiers.

I duck my head in contrition.

"I think it went well, Sarge," Lance says mildly before tugging on his shirt.

"No one fucking asked you." Rafe points up the hill. "Move out, now."

Lance shrugs on his pack and obeys.

Rafe points to me. "We're going to talk about this," he promises.

Four hours later, we're back at HQ, an empty airplane hangar. Soon a tiny charter plane will show up to secret us back home. Lance helped me hose off the blood—my wolf was reluctant to remove all traces of its kills. I went for a run first, trying to rid myself of the pent-up energy, waiting until the last possible minute to shift.

Channing arrives at HQ last and doesn't bother with the hose. He sticks his head in a bucket of water and then uses a rag to wipe off his face paint. "The package was delivered safely," he announces. "All's well that ends well."

"Not so fucking fast." Rafe marches back into the hangar from the outside, where he was taking a call from command. "We've got a problem." My alpha rounds on me and points. "Your wolf is out of control, Deke." He's not wrong. I disobeyed a direct order.

"Yes, Sergeant." My voice is gravely, guttural, as if my throat is unused to human words. We still call Rafe Sarge even though we're no longer in the Army.

"Did you have orders to kill, Deke?"

A sick feeling roils in my belly. This is why Rafe decided we needed to get out of the service last year. Every hunt, I was becoming more feral. We all were. Rafe said we had to leave before we all lost our humanity and needed to be put down.

"In Deke's defense, he only killed the Tangos," Channing offers.

Rafe bares his teeth at Channing, who ducks his head and puts up his hands in surrender.

"We didn't have kill orders," Rafe growls.

"Colonel Johnson wouldn't contract us if he didn't expect a body count," Lance counters.

"That's only because Deke's out of control," Rafe shouts.

The weight on my chest increases.

Fuck.

Rafe paces, his boots striking the concrete floor in a staccato beat. Rafe can glide silently if he wants to. He's making noise now to make a point. I brace myself for it.

It comes all too soon. Rafe stops in front of me and blows on the dog whistle. I stand at attention, fighting not to cringe at the high pitched sound. Channing and Lance snap their hands over their ears.

"What does that mean, soldier?" Rafe barks at me.

"All systems go, sir!" I shout back.

Rafe blows the dog whistle again, two short blasts. "And that?"

"Abort mission, sir!"

Rafe gets right in my face, yellow eyes fixed on mine. I stare off in the distance, fighting my wolf's restless urge to break position and attack.

This is a test. If I break position and challenge my alpha, it's a sign I'm way too far gone. Something my pack has been worried about for a couple years now.

I have to pass this test.

I force myself to think of puppies. Innocent toddlers. Human females—that's a new thought, but for some reason it comes to mind. Like I might reward myself for passing this test by seeking out pleasure.

As if.

My team won't let me near humans. Not after that bar fight last year. My wolf is way too aggressive and unpredictable. Too bloodthirsty.

But the thought of fragile creatures is enough. My wolf relaxes.

My alpha stands inches away. He senses the change in my body and nods. But he doesn't let me off the hook.

"Discipline, soldier," Rafe growls right in my ringing ear. "It's all that stands between us and moon madness."

I unclench my jaw. "Yes, sir."

CHAPTER 2

*adie*

Sadie, are you heading to the plaza? I'll be there too. Let's catch up after your girls' night. The text beeps through on my phone and makes my stomach twist into a dense knot. The message may sound friendly, but it registers in my body as an assault.

I am so done with Scott Sears and his attempts to win me back.

What part of "it's over" did he not get?

I roll my eyes and shove my phone back in my purse, shifting my ridiculous but precious package back under my arm as I duck through the crowded Taos restaurant after work.

It's dinner time on a school night, and while most nights I'd rather go home and chill after teaching kindergarteners all day, it's Wednesday.

Whine Wednesday, as me and my girl posse like to call it, and Whine Wednesdays are sacred.

"Sadie, over here." Adele waves from her seat at a table on the patio. The knotted muscles in my neck relax a hair when I see her and the rest of my friends. Tabitha and Charlie slouch in their chairs but sit up a little straighter when they see me. Adele remains sitting with her back ramrod straight.

My friends are the best. We're all different, but it works.

Adele's the polished, always-put-together Creole beauty who owns the local chocolate shop. She's our mother hen, and always looks perfect in her vintage clothes. Tonight she's in a 1950s style swing dress, the moss green color perfectly complementing her golden brown skin and green eyes. Instead of a jacket, she wears a shawl in taupe with gold thread. She's the fancy one in the group, and she owns it.

Tabitha often wears vintage clothes too, either from the 1920s or 60s and 70s. Somehow she pulls off a sequined flapper dress one day, giant bell bottoms the next. Today she lounges loose-limbed in her chair with a beaded headband and a yellow jumpsuit. Another one of her Cher outfits, and she looks the part with her olive skin and narrow face.

Charlie is Charlie. She's the shortest of us and the most fit. Most of the time, I see her in a blue button down shirt and sturdy navy shorts or pants—her post mistress outfit. Her job gives her a perpetual tan that matches her short blond hair. Right now she's wearing a faded t-shirt that reads "In my defense, I was left unsupervised."

And me, I'm just Sadie Diaz, Taos native. Kindergarten teacher, brown eyes, brown hair. Average height, average weight, average everything. Tabitha tells me I dress like a kindergarten teacher, whatever that means. The kids love my kitty earrings and brightly colored ballet flats.

"Glad you made it," Charlie smiles at me. She's already

got a margarita in front of her, and I try not to look too jealous.

"Sorry I'm late," I say and swing my bag off my shoulder. "I had to pick up a package."

Tabitha grimaces at the black toy box I set on the restaurant table. "What the hell is that?" Her voice is loud enough to make several fellow restaurant goers swivel their heads to our table, but she doesn't care. She leans back, nose wrinkled as she regards the toy.

I get why she's making a face. The stuffed toy inside is a cross between a demon and a jackrabbit, with red eyes, antlers and fangs.

"It's a jackalope," I say, my tone apologetic. All three of my best friends lean in to inspect the toy box.

"Oh I've heard of these." Charlie picks up the box and wrinkles her nose as she reads the back print. "It's the hottest toy this year. Sold out in most states."

"I ordered mine nine months ago," I admit. "The kids in my class can't stop talking about it. There are parents willing to commit murder to get one for their kids. That's why I have it here. It just came in, and I'm not letting it out of my sight."

"How does this work? Oh yes." Charlie pushes a red button marked, *Try me!* on the clear plastic, and creepy laughter echoes from the box. The monstrous toy shakes, and its red eyes flash. "Don't you want to play?" it mocks in a voice straight from *Poltergeist.*

"Holy shit!" Tabitha chokes. "What the hell?"

"Oh, hell no." Adele shakes her head, so her soft brown curls bounce around her face as she holds up a hand. "That is too creepy." She shivers and tugs her shawl around her. With the sun going down, it's getting cool.

"It *is* creepy." I examine the toy more closely. "The first time I pressed the button, I almost dropped the box. And I knew it did that."

"Press it again," Tabitha says with a wicked grin. Adele rolls her eyes.

"You sure?" Charlie hovers her thumb over the button.

"Do it," Tabitha has a maniacal look not unlike the demon jackalope.

Gritting her teeth, Charlie pushes it. "*Don't you want to play*?" a sinister voice whispers from the toy box.

"Oh!" Adele and Tabitha both cry. "Put it away," Adele orders. Tabitha looks like she wants to push the button again.

"Shit," Charlie says emphatically and places the box at arm's length away from her on the table. "Kids really like to play with this stuff?"

I shrug.

"Kids these days," Adele says, straightening her silverware beside the empty place where her plate will go for the fifth time. "Way more into scary stuff than I ever was."

"At least it's not baby Cthulhu. Those were super in last year," I say. The waitress bustles up with her tray full of our drinks, and I take the toy and carefully set the box back in my bag.

"So you got one for your class?" Adele asks.

"Yeah. Only one, so they'll have to share."

"You are the nicest kindergarten teacher ever." Tabitha salutes me with her strawberry margarita. "And that's saying something. That bar is high."

"To Sweet Sadie," Charlie raises her Fat Tire in toast.

"Sadie," Tabitha and Adele join in, raising their glasses.

I flush and sip my mango margarita with them. My friends are the best thing in my life right now. I love them like sisters, even though we couldn't be more different.

"You didn't want a margarita?" Tabitha asks Adele.

"No," Adele sniffs and swirls her red wine in the glass.

"They're really good," Tabitha singsongs and flips her long, straight red hair over her shoulder.

"No thank you." Adele tips the glass, closing her eyes and swirling her wine to inhale the bouquet.

"Snob," Tabitha mocks gently.

"Leave her alone." Charlie's voice is a little loud, but it's not the alcohol talking. Charlie just likes to be loud. She balances her chair on its back two legs for a second then lets it fall to all fours with a thud. "Someone should be drinking wine," she pronounces. "It is *Wine* Wednesday."

"You mean Whine Wednesday," Tabitha corrects. "We agreed when we started this tradition we don't actually have to drink wine, we just have to whine. So who's going first?"

"Sadie." Adele's green eyes pierce me over her wine glass. She sees everything, and she's our unofficial mother hen.

"Sadie? Everything all right?" Tabitha asks.

"Who do I have to kill?" Charlie adds and plants her elbows on the table. "Is it Scott? I will fuck him up." She means it too.

"Everything's fine." I sigh and set down my margarita.

"Nope, come on, spill." Tabitha waves her fingers in a come hither motion. "What's Scott up to now?"

"Are you guys back together?" Charlie's brow furrows. "I thought after... The Incident…"

"The Incident? Is that what we're calling cheating now?" Tabitha runs her finger around the rim of her margarita, collecting the salt.

"We're still broken up," I say. "But he wants me back. He just texted again, asking if we could meet tonight."

"Seriously? He cheated on you!" Both Charlie and Tabitha explode.

"Shhh." Adele lifts a hand. "Calm down, Sadie's talking."

"Thanks." I give her a small smile. "We're not getting back together. I told him no, but he's being really persistent." I glance down at my phone in my bag. I turned it off after that last text to get some peace. At any given moment, I could have several missed calls and unread texts from Scott.

"Persistent how?" Tabitha asks, her eyes narrowed.

"Texts, phone calls," I tell my friends. "Gifts. He sent flowers, chocolates."

"Did he get the chocolates from The Chocolatier?" Charlie asks Adele.

Adele shakes her head, still looking at me. "No. He knows if he comes into my store, I'll roast him alive." She says it delicately, but I have no doubt in a run-in between Scott and Adele, Adele would win.

"Okay, so Scott brought you *subpar* chocolate," Tabitha says, emphasizing *subpar* as if this is the most egregious sin. And in our group, it is egregious. "Then what?"

"He just won't stop reaching out. The other day, he and my dad were outside the school. Scott said it was for a development meeting, but I think he planned it right when I would take my kids out for recess."

"Gross," Charlie says.

"That is just like Scott. So shady. Why doesn't your dad see it?" Tabitha fretts.

"Because Sadie's dad is the same," Adele says firmly. "Birds of a feather." She looks me right in the eye and raises a slim brown brow.

I keep silent because she's right. My dad loves Scott and his development ideas way more than I ever did. He has our marriage all planned, so then, the two of them can take over all the real estate in the area. Adele is right. Scott is a carbon copy of my dad.

"You're going to resist, right?" Tabitha bites her lip. "You won't take him back?"

"No." I have no intention of letting Scott in ever again. "But he won't stop. You know he won't just take no for an answer."

"Gross," Charlie says again and drains her beer. The rest of us finish our drinks too, and when the waitress comes by, we all order another with our food.

"Can we help?" Tabitha asks once the waitress is gone. "Maybe we can talk to him."

"No, don't do that. Knowing Scott, it'll make things worse. He's just used to getting what he wants."

"You can't trust these real estate developer types," Charlie says around a mouthful of tortilla chips. "So pushy. They make deals all day and then come home and think that's the only way to relate to another person."

Tabitha agrees, and she and Charlie launch into one of the Taoseños' favorite topics: the evil real estate developer.

"I'm sorry, Sadie," Adele says quietly to me.

"It's okay. Let's talk about something else. I don't want my crappy relationship stuff to ruin our night out."

Adele squeezes my hand but doesn't say anything

Fortunately, I'm saved by the roar of motorcycles across the plaza. Four big bikes manned by giant bikers roll up to the plaza and stop in an alleyway next to the pedestrian only area.

"Oh jeez," Tabitha groans. "More *Easy Rider* fans recreating their journey through the Southwest." Ever since the iconic sixties film, bikers have made Taos part of their pilgrimage. That's in addition to the huge annual biker rally up in Red River over Memorial Day that brings over 20,000 bikers to the area.

Something about these guys is different, though. They don't look like *Easy Rider* hippie types. Nor do they have the long beards or hair that goes with some biker gangs. These guys are huge and fit. Broad shoulders and barrel chests. Thick, muscled thighs.

Oh God, am I looking at their thighs?

We fall silent as they dismount and file past the restaurant window. They *are* covered in leather and tattoos, like you'd expect, and all of them wear aviator shades.

"Damn," Tabitha murmurs, slouching lower in her chair.

"Yikes. I'll bet if you brush up against one of those guys, you'll get testosterone poisoning," Charlie sniffs. The four bikers pause right in front of the restaurant patio. They stand in a badass cluster, talking.

One of them isn't wearing a leather jacket, just a black leather vest that leaves his arms bare. When he pulls off his aviator shades, his biceps bulge, practically as big as a basketball. The tattoo on his arm—a black wolf under a full moon—ripples, and the muscles in my lower belly clench, hard.

The biker who just removed his sunglasses swivels his head slowly in our direction. He's got dark hair buzzed into a crew cut, leaving nothing to mar the masculine lines of his face. Wowza. His coffee-dark eyes flash weirdly in the dusky light. A jolt runs through my limbs. He's looking straight at me.

My hand, of its own volition, rises into the air.

"Sadie!" Tabitha whisper-shouts. "What are you doing?"

I honestly don't know. I can't seem to look away from the guy, who is about as much my type as the lamppost behind him. Still, I give a little wave. The biker jerks up his chin in salute. A shock of electricity runs through me, tip to toe, like I've been struck by a mini bolt of lightning. The man's perfect lips twitch into the hint of a smirk, and he turns back to his buddies.

The biker guys finish their conversation and stride away. Their heavy boots make no sound on the stones, but the air of the square seems to crackle. The dark haired biker looks back, right at me, and winks. Another zap, and my heart trips over itself.

"Wait… did that guy just *wink* at you?" Adele exclaims.

I laugh. "Yes, I believe he did."

"Oh sweet baby Jesus," Tabitha groans.

"Those guys are scary," Charlie jerks her thumb over her shoulder.

"I don't know," I muse. "I thought he was kinda hot." Scott was tall and handsome, and prided himself on his gym made muscles. But stand Scott next to that dark haired biker, and my ex would look like a bobble head toy.

My friends' mouths drop at my admission, and then we all dissolve into girlish laughter.

I look out the window to see where they went.

"Who are those motorcycle guys?" Tabitha asks the waitress when she comes with our food.

The woman shrugs. "I see them around here from time to time. Sometimes on their bikes, sometimes in one of those army looking trucks."

"Seriously? A Humvee?" Charlie's eyebrows climb. She knows cars.

"Is a Humvee like a Hummer?" Tabitha asks.

"No, it's a military vehicle," Charlie answers. "Not all of them are road legal. Are those guys former military?"

"I don't ask, honey," the waitress says. "I keep my mouth shut and look my fill."

"See," I point out. "She thinks they're hot, too."

"I didn't say they weren't hot," Tabitha mumbles, taking a drink of water.

"Do they ever eat here?" Adele asks. Her water glass is half full, and she's still clutching it.

"No, they don't stick around long. When they're not on their bikes, they load up on supplies and head out," the waitress says.

Charlie taps her lips. "I thought they looked more military than biker gang. The way they stood, you know? Shoulders back and chests up. And their buzzcuts."

"I was just looking at the one with the wolf and moon tattoo," I confess.

"They all had wolf and moon tattoos," Adele says.

"Really?" Tabitha squints at Adele.

"Yes." Adele doesn't say anything further.

"Can you imagine Sadie showing up with a guy like that as her new boyfriend? Scott would shit a brick," Charlie says.

"So would her dad," Tabitha agrees.

Adele chokes on her laugh. "Oh god, that would be hilarious. Can you imagine the look on Scott's face?"

It's my turn to grab my water and drink deeply. I can just imagine Scott's face if he saw me next to a biker man like that. He'd throw a fit. But I don't want to think about Scott. What would it be like to date a guy like the biker? Would he be great in bed? Assuming he'd look twice at me. That kind of guy, those muscles, bare and sleek spread out on my comforter…

A flush spreads over my face. I clutch my empty water glass. There's not enough water in the world to quench this desire.

"I was just kidding," Charlie says with an alarmed look my way. Like she's guessed at my thoughts. How far I've run down the road of trying on that giant man as a partner. "I was totally kidding. Those guys definitely aren't safe."

"If they're military, they're probably a lot safer than a biker gang," I reason.

Charlie shakes her head. "Even if they are, they're trouble. I would never date a military guy. They are man-whores and adrenaline junkies. Definitely not boyfriend material. Especially not for you."

"What is that supposed to mean?" I demand.

"No, nothing. Just that you're sweet, Sadie. I only suggested it to be funny. I figured you'd never, ever date a guy who looked like them."

I shrug my shoulders. "Well, you never know."

My friends all give me sharp glances, and I wink to make them laugh again, but something rebellious and bold has taken root inside me.

I sort of love the idea of shocking every resident in this small town who thinks they know me by hanging around a big, bad biker.

But Charlie's right. That's just nuts.

~

Deke

THERE'S a sweet scent wafting across the town plaza. It's driving my wolf crazy. I keep raising my head and sniffing the air.

"Cut it out," Lance mutters to me, and a growl rumbles in my chest. My blond packmate is standing too close. Fucker's doing it on purpose. He knows my wolf needs space.

"Leave him alone," Channing defends me to Lance. "It's almost a full moon. That makes him crazy."

"This is Deke we're talking about," Lance retorts. "He's always crazy."

I narrow my eyes at him, my growl intensifying. Lance side steps quickly, dancing out of the way. I've been known to up and punch my packmates for less provocation.

"No fighting." Rafe, our Alpha, emerges from the alley shadows. "Not in front of civilians." By *civilians* he means *humans*. Rafe glowers extra long at Lance. The two are brothers, but Rafe never plays favorites. If anything, he's harder on Lance than us.

"Business done?" Lance asks, running a hand through his surfer blond hair. Fucking pretty boy preens like he's in a boy band.

"Yep, let's move out," Rafe orders.

The other guys immediately follow our alpha. But I resist, scuffing my boots on the plaza stones. That scent calls to me. Candy sweet. My mouth waters.

Rafe doesn't miss my reluctance. "Deke? You coming?"

"I don't know." I rub my chin. "I think I might stay a while." Even as I say it, I know it's lame. I'm the last of my pack who'd want to stick around a public plaza crawling with humans. Things are better for me now that I'm out of the service. We have our own place and can run free in the mountains every night. It keeps my wolf manageable. But I'm still the guy who gets edgy around too many people.

"For what? There's no band tonight." Channing smirks and points to an old concert flyer. "And I didn't know you liked Jimmy Buffett."

I flip him the bird.

"Deke," Rafe says, a hint of growl in his voice.

"What?" Out of respect for my alpha, I tuck my middle finger away. "I just want to stay out a little longer. Enjoy the night air."

There's a long pause while my pack stares at me like I announced I wanted to put on a pretty pink tutu and dance a *pas de deux*.

"I could stay," Lance offers.

"I don't need a babysitter." Enough of this fucker. I bare my teeth. In answer, Lance's wolf makes its presence known, eyes flashing blue. My wolf surges to the fore, a second away from snapping its chain.

"Fine." Rafe steps between me and his brother, inserting himself physically. Ever the peacemaker, until we piss him off too far. Then he kicks our asses. Not a perfect system, but it works. "Deke, you do what you want. The rest of us are heading back." He jerks his head, and Channing and Lance march to the bikes. Rafe hangs back.

"You sure about this?" he mutters to me. My alpha's the only one who has the right to ask this question, and it still makes me bristle. I don't have the best track record around humans. I'm not charming, like Lance. I get downright surly, and if provoked… well, let's just say trouble is guaranteed

Rafe knows this, and he keeps a closer eye on me. If he were a lesser wolf, my wolf would challenge him and rip him to shreds.

Most of the time, I'm glad Rafe is a better fighter than me. If I ever lost control or went too far, he'd be there to put me down.

But tonight, I want to be left alone. "I'm good," I say and stretch my lips in a semblance of a smile. This is my happy face, and I know it leaves a lot to be desired. I've been told skeletons are less creepy.

Sure enough, Rafe shakes his head. "Don't show that to civilians. You'll scare them," he orders, but then he slaps my arm in universal bro code for "Take care," and leaves me, heading in the direction of the bikes.

A sigh heaves outta me when my pack rides away. Normally, I'd be glad to get away from this town and all these people. Happy to be on the motorcycle. There's nothing like a long ride on the mountain roads, the wind rushing over me and chilling my arms, nothing between me and the night sky. But tonight, I've got more important things to do than ride.

I lift my head to the moon and drink in the candy sweetness. I'm gonna find the owner of this sweet scent before my wolf goes crazy—crazier than he already is.

Sadie

I'm quiet for the rest of Whine Wednesday. I leave the whining to my friends, and, a little after sunset, I bow out early.

"School night," I tell the ladies as I say my goodbyes.

As I cross the plaza, I turn on my phone. It buzzes with all the missed texts and calls. Two voicemails from Scott. One from my dad. I don't know which message I dread more.

At least the night is pretty. The sun has sunk below the horizon, leaving a haze of twilight blue. I thought about leaving Taos, running away like my mom did. But I don't want to leave my hometown. Besides, I'm more like my father than I care to admit. Stubborn. I might be quiet and sweet, but I don't like to lose.

A few more text messages pop up on my screen. From Scott, *Where are you?* And then, *I know it's Wine Wednesday.* He spelled it wrong, even though I've told him about the pun repeatedly. A simple detail, and he can't bother—or doesn't care. It makes me grit my teeth. It wouldn't bother me, but

Scott always looked down on my friends. They were polite enough to him in support of me, but I wish I had let Adele tear him a new one.

I start to order a rideshare home—I don't drive my car into town on Wednesdays since I know I'll be drinking—but before I can confirm, a text from Scott comes through that makes a chill run down my body. *I see you're at Lizanos. I'm here in the plaza, by the Rideshare pick up spot. Let's talk.*

Oh no. I hustle forward, but I'm too late. I see the blue sign and sure enough, there he is—a tall, lanky man in black slacks and a sleek athleisure wear jacket. Scott. He's got his bluetooth headset on, and by the way he's gesturing, I can tell he's talking to someone on the phone. Probably making a deal to raze a hundred year old adobe church and put in a bunch of condos and a strip mall.

I halt and step behind a small hut that's a permanent market stall. I could go back to my friends and ask for an escort to the rideshare area, but with several drinks in them, at least one of them will insist on confronting Scott. And the other two will join in, and it'll be a scene.

What am I going to do?

A strange green light flashes at me from the alleyway. A dark shape slouches in the shadows. As I watch, it straightens, growing taller and enormous, as a giant man emerges. It's the biker guy from earlier, the one who winked at me. I recognize him even in the dark. He's got his shades propped on his head. His eyes are dark brown but catching the light in a weird way—flashing green. He's looking right at me.

Can you imagine Sadie showing up with a guy like that?

I clutch my cardigan closed. I have a wild, crazy idea, and before I lose my nerve, I walk over to him.

Scary biker dude is even bigger up close. He's got dog tags on a chain around his neck. Military, like Charlie said.

I lick my lips. I can't even believe I'm doing this. "Excuse me," I call to him. My voice comes out squeaky. I clear my throat and try again. "Excuse me. Can you help me with something?"

He steps forward like he was just waiting for my invitation. His head cocks to the side, and his perfect lips part. "Yeah, sweetheart?" His voice is deep and soft. Normally, I hate being called *sweetheart*, but his eyes are on my face. His nostrils flare like he's breathing me in, and his eyes seem to turn even more green.

His intense regard is a little unnerving.

"Um," I squeak again. "I've got a problem."

"Problem?" he echoes.

"Yeah. It's not that big of a deal, but I was hoping you could help me." This is crazy. This is nuts. This is the boldest thing I've ever done, and I'll probably never have the nerve to do again. Maybe it's the mango margarita talking, or maybe it's just me being brave for once.

"Sure thing, sweetheart." Biker man agrees so quickly I lose my train of thought.

"You don't even know what it is." I gaze up into his brown eyes and get a little dizzy.

He shrugs. "Try me."

"Okay. There's this guy," I say in rush. "He's actually my ex, and he's kinda bothering me. He tracked me down somehow, and he's over there, waiting for me." I point to the rideshare parking spot.

The biker peers around the corner. A low, rumbling sound seems to emit from his chest. The biker turns back to me, and the sound abruptly cuts off. "You want me to kill him?"

"No." I giggle at the joke. Because it has to be a joke, even if the man sounds dead serious. "Silly." I shake my head at him like he's one of my kindergarten students.

A grin forms at the corners of his lips, and I feel warm all over.

"You sure, sweetheart?" Now there's a hint of teasing in his voice.

"Yeah." I play along. "It's too public here. And where would we even hide the body?"

The guy scratches his chin. "We could figure something out. You could lure him somewhere. Somewhere remote. And I could make it look like a wolf finished him off."

"Um, okay." *That is weirdly specific.* I pretend to think about it. "Nah, not necessary. I just want him to back off. I was just thinking you could walk me over there and pretend to be my date. Just for a few minutes."

"Your date," he repeats.

Oh God. It was a stupid idea. I'm embarrassing myself horribly here.

"That's what you want?" The man raises a dark brow.

Here it comes, my blush, rolling up from my chest. Fortunately it's night, and the dim plaza lights should hide my bright red face. "If you don't mind."

"I don't know."

"That's okay." I want to turn away to escape this humiliation, but the biker ducks his head close. He smells like leather and clean male skin. My senses tingle. "Seems more efficient to make it permanent." I can tell by his tone he's joking.

I let out a hysterical giggle. "Could you do it my way?" I whisper back. "As a favor?"

"A favor, huh?" He tucks a bit of hair behind my ear. At his touch, my legs go wobbly, and I lean back against the building.

It occurs to me that approaching a huge and scary-looking man in a dark alleyway was probably not my brightest move. What made me think he was safer than Scott? But I can't find it in me to be afraid. The flutters in my belly, the ratcheting of my pulse—they aren't from fear. No, they're from excitement.

"What's your name?" I ask over the pitter-patter of my heartbeat.

"Deke. Yours?"

"Sadie."

"Sadie," he murmurs in his deep voice. He rests an arm above me. For a moment, his big body cages me against the wall.

I'm still not scared.

Instead, I feel small and safe, hidden from the world.

Then he steps away. "Okay, Sadie. Let's do this."

~

Sadie

I SENSE Deke's big hand hovering at the small of my back as I stroll across the plaza with him at my side. Deke's twice as big as me and almost twice as tall, but when he walks he makes no sound.

"My ex's name is Scott," I tell him as we walk toward the drop off spot.

"Scott." Deke's lip curls.

"We dated for three years." I don't know why I'm babbling, but I can't stop. "I don't know why I was with him so long. He was nice in the beginning, but…"

Deke's broad chest vibrates with another rumbling sound. Automatically, I put my hand on his shoulder, and the sound cuts off. He stops in his tracks, and so do I, turning to face him.

"He didn't hurt me," I clarify. "We broke it off when I found out he was cheating on me. But now he wants me back."

"And you, Sadie?" Deke studies me in a way that sends little shivers up and down my spine. "What do you want?"

My heart sighs at the question. When was the last time a man asked me what I want? "I want him to leave me alone."

"And then what?" We're face to face and chest to chest, close enough I can feel his heat soaking into my skin. There's an ache growing in my lower belly, a deep hunger I haven't felt in far too long.

"I want to be happy. I want to be free."

Deke puts his hand on my arm, and for a moment, it's just the two of us. His fingers circle my forearm and slide down, shackling my wrist. His thumb brushes over my pulse, and I'm this close to giving up our mission and finding a dark corner to explore the promise of this stranger's touch.

Then I hear Scott's voice echoing across the parking lot. He's on the phone but not bothering to keep his side of the conversation quiet. He always did that, even when we were at home, as if he wanted to make sure everyone within twenty feet knew how important his call was.

I turn, but Deke doesn't let go. He slides his hand down further to take my hand and thread his fingers with mine. My heart hammers at the excitement of it. The audacity of holding a stranger's hand so intimately. It feels wild and rebellious and fun. I smile up at him, and his lips kick up a bit at the corners. We walk the rest of the parking lot like that, hand in hand.

Oh God, I hope I haven't made a mistake. I pick up my pace and trot out a little ahead as we approach my ex.

Scott sees me and pivots. "Sadie." He touches his headset and loudly tells the caller he has to go, instead of making me wait five minutes for the call to end naturally—like he used to do when we were dating. He gives me his toothpaste commercial smile as if to say *See, baby? See how important you are to me?* I resist the urge to roll my eyes.

Then Scott notices Deke, and his eyes narrow. It's so obvious what he's thinking. *Another man on my turf.*

I brace myself for a pissing contest. Not exactly a proud moment for me, using another man to intimidate my ex. But then Deke squeezes my hand and steps forward to face Scott, and I realize just how small and plastic-looking Scott is. Fake tan and perfect hair. He looks like a Ken doll next to a souped up G.I. Joe.

I'm going to enjoy this.

"Scott," I say. "I got your texts. All of them."

"Sadie." Scott looks down his nose at Deke. An impressive feat, considering Deke is taller than him. "Is this a friend?"

"Nope," Deke says. "I'm Sadie's new man." And he drapes his arm around my shoulders. I step close and lean against his chest. His very firm, muscular chest.

"This is Deke. We just met, and…well, we hit it off." I smile up at Deke. Our gaze locks for an extra long second, and I forget to breath. Wow, he really is stunning.

I almost forget Scott is standing right in front of us. He clears his throat three times before I return my attention to him. Scott's nose wrinkles like he smelled something rotten. "Sadie, this isn't like you."

I give him a mock innocent expression. "What isn't?"

"I mean… you just met? You're holding this guy's hand?" He gives his head a shake, like he's trying to erase the whole thing from his mind. "I was hoping we could talk. Alone."

I stay quiet, and Deke squeezes me gently. I realize my

fake biker boyfriend is waiting for my cue. He's going to let me stand up for myself first.

"That's not necessary. It's over, Scott. I've moved on."

"Sadie—" Scott steps forward, and that rumbling sound comes from Deke's chest again. It's a growl. A *literal* growl.

Scott freezes midstep.

"Take a hint, Sears," Deke uses Scott's last name. Maybe Deke knows Scott better than I thought. "She's over you. Listen to what Sadie's telling you and move on."

Scott starts to sputter, and Deke gently turns me, so our backs are to my ex. "Ready, babe?" Deke asks me.

"Yes," I say, though I have no idea what he's talking about. He keeps me nestled in the crook of his arm as he walks me back across the plaza towards his bike. When we reach the giant motorcycle, he releases me. Out of the corner of my eye, I see that Scott still watching us.

"Here." Deke hands me something. A black helmet.

"What's this for?" I ask.

"Your head." Humor laces his tone. "You want to go for a ride? Just to rile him up?"

My eyes go wide, but I nod. *Yes, yes I do.*

He takes the helmet and puts it on for me, adjusting it to my head and fastening it carefully. My heart goes *tha-thump* as he fusses over the strap, his big fingers surprisingly nimble. He unlatches the side saddlebag and motions for me to hand him my big bag with the jackalope. When I do, he sets it in the leather case and threads the belt-like lock. Then he swings onto the bike, kicking up the stand and steadying it. "Hop on."

Ok, this is happening. He wants me on the bike. I picked a biker for a fake boyfriend, and now I'm about to ride off with him with my ex watching.

Deke turns on the bike and revs it. The air shivers with the engine's roar.

"Ready, babe?" he calls over the noise.

I'm not sure if he's calling me babe in case Scott hears or if he's just calling me babe because that's what he calls women, but it makes me smile.

I take a deep breath and swing on behind him. He takes my hands and locks them around his front. I grab a handful of his soft t-shirt and feel a thrill at the hard muscles underneath.

I can't believe I'm doing this.

"Okay?" Deke calls over his shoulder. His cheek is curved into a grin. He's not wearing a helmet.

"You're not wearing a helmet," I say. I sound like a prissy kindergarten teacher, even to my ears.

"Babe," he says in reply, and the bike takes off with a roar. We ride right past Scott. I can't see his face, but I can imagine his stunned rage. It is delicious. I give a little wave in his direction and then grip Deke tighter as we fly up the main drag of town—Paseo del Pueblo Norte road—and around the curve into the open night.

I never knew riding a motorcycle was so much fun. The night air is crisp and rushes all around us. Deke's bike is a monster of leather and chrome, purring hot under me, but Deke's even bigger. He rides with perfect ease, his big body solid and upright, blocking most of the wind. I press against him, my cheek to his leather vest. He doesn't go too far out of town, turning down a back road to loop back. When he leans into turns, I lean with him, and the bike twines nimbly up and down the back roads of Taos.

For a moment, I think about shouting a few questions —"Where are we going? What's the plan?"—but the sky is so vast above us, black velvet studded with diamond stars, and the night is so big and boundless, I forgot my concerns.

There's nothing but the giant man I'm holding onto, the bike rumbling under the both of us and the endless roads. Worries about work, Scott, my friends and what the hell I am doing fall away. I leave them behind like old hubcaps and alligator strips on the side of the road.

I am happy. I am free.

Deke guides the bike over a one-lane bridge and stops. I look at the babbling river just below—a tributary of the Rio Grande. Above us, through the treetops, a million stars glitter in the dark sky. It's dark and secluded, but I'm not afraid.

"This is nice," I say.

"Yeah." His voice is soft. He looms over me, large but not imposing. The night air is chilly, and I should be cold, but all I feel is the heat emanating off him. Another step, and I'd be in his arms.

I met this guy less than an hour ago, and already I've been on his bike. I put my arms around him and held on tight. And now I'm out here, alone, just me and a stranger who already seems like a friend.

I'm perfectly content until I realize what my friends would say.

I just got on the back of a stranger's motorcycle and let him drive away with me. Into the dark. Without any discussion of where he was going or how I would get home.

Deke

THE LITTLE HUMAN gazes up at me, biting her lip. The wind kicks up, carrying her candy scent to me. I can't get enough of it. She is literally the cutest human I've ever met. Everything about her makes me want to smile. And I haven't smiled in ages.

Now that I'm alone with Sadie, the constant noise I usually tolerate from my wolf has died down. That urge toward violence—the underlying restlessness—seems to have dropped away. It's been replaced by the urge to mark her, but that feeling I can control.

I won't go there with sweet Sadie Diaz. I know claiming a human is an impossibility for me.

I'm way too far gone. Too dangerous.

"Um, thanks for helping me with that," Sadie says.

"No problem. Happy to help." I would've done it anyway. I wish I could've done more, and if I'd met Scott alone, maybe I would have. As it turned out, I acted pretty civilized. My pack would be shocked.

"I never thought Scott would be like this." Sadie shakes her head. I hate hearing his name on her lips, but I'm glad she's confiding in me. I'm happy to let her talk. "What I don't get is how he knew where I was. He's stalking me somehow."

Now this I can do something about. "Phone," I order and hold out my hand, palm up. She tilts her head at me, her brow wrinkling.

"Let me see your phone," I clarify. I've gotta remember to speak in full sentences. Most of the time I don't bother. I hate people and speaking in monosyllables is a good way to communicate my contempt. It drives my pack crazy, which is a bonus.

She pulls her phone out of her jeans pocket and hands it to me.

"Password?"

"No password," she says.

"Seriously? You need a password." I swipe to the security

set up and have her put in a password. "Nothing too easy to guess," I lecture. "No common dates or birthdays."

"Fine." She pretends to complain but types something in.

"You got one?" I ask, and she nods. "Good. What is it?"

She frowns at me before she realizes I'm joking. "Like I'd tell you," she retorts playfully.

"Good girl." I give her a half grin then get her to unlock the phone for me. I search only a second before I spot the tracking app. I show the screen to her. "Did Scott ask you to install this app?"

Her eyes get wide. "What is that?"

"It's an app that broadcasts your phone's location to anyone you invite."

"I didn't install that. Scott never asked me to install anything," Sadie says.

Fucker. Maybe I will kill him. I can't have my wolf do it now that I shared that plan with Sadie. I'll have to think up something else.

"He probably did it without asking then. It would be easy because you didn't have a password." I type with my thumb as I talk, uninstalling the app. "I'm getting rid of it. When you get home, back up your data and do a hard reset. Keep the password and restart your phone every morning. The best offense is a good defense."

I also enter my phone number. "I'm putting my number in here in case you need a rescue again. Is that okay?"

"Yes. Thank you." Sadie accepts the phone back and squints up at me. "How do you know all this?"

"I'm in security."

"Like cyber security?" The wind ruffles her hair, and I step closer to shield her from it.

"All types of security. But mostly government security missions." This is the longest conversation I've had with a human in years. I'd never willingly offer this information up to anyone, but Sadie is different. Sadie is special. "My partners and I own Black Wolf Security."

"Oh!" Her eyes sparkle. "Is that why you all have wolf tattoos?"

I rock back on my heels. "You noticed that?"

"My friend did. I only noticed yours."

My dick stirs against my zipper. My wolf likes that she picked me out of the pack. "We all got them before we left the army." I push up my sleeve and show her my biceps. "We were Special Ops."

She traces the moon with light fingertips. Electricity shoots through me, and I lean closer to catch the vanilla scent in her hair. She's pale skinned and luminous in the moonlight, her silky hair wafting around her face. Normally, I hate being touched, but my wolf would happily stretch out for a belly rub.

"It's nice." She fingers my tattoo. Is her voice deeper, husky? Is it the night air?

She pulls her hand away, and I have to swallow several times. My cock is a hard bar, pressing against the front of my jeans. "What about you?" I ask, my own voice deeper than normal to my ears. "What do you do?"

"I teach kindergarten. Which reminds me, I should get home. It's a school night."

"Did you leave your car in the plaza? Or do you want me to take you home?"

She nibbles her lip. I think the stop made her nervous. Which is good. She shouldn't just hop on the back of a random guy's motorcycle and ride around town with him. Still, I hate the thought of her being afraid of me.

"Home, please."

"Sure. Give me the address." The least I can do is see her safely home.

I savor each second of the ride to her condo north of Taos. She squeezes me closer every time I lean into a turn. I take the final miles slower, easing into each turn, enjoying the night-painted landscape instead of speeding by. The shadows and midnight blue.

I pull up to her door and plant my feet to steady my bike but stay facing forward, shoulders rigid. This wasn't a date—it was a rescue op. My job was to get the package to her place. Not to walk her to the door. Definitely not to lean down to savor that delicious scent before she goes inside.

For a moment, Sadie doesn't move. She's still holding me as if reluctant to disentangle herself. I grit my teeth and try not to think how easily she could slide her hand down my stomach, into my jeans. My cock jerks at the thought.

Finally, she slips off the bike. I lose the battle with myself and turn my head slightly to fill my senses with her vanilla scent.

"Thanks for the ride," she says. "And, um, everything." She removes my helmet and hands it to me. I swap her purse for it. She slings her bag over her shoulder but still makes no move to go.

"Are you going to be in town tomorrow for Plaza Live?" she asks after a moment of fidgeting. "The Flying Oysters are playing at six. They mostly do covers, but they're pretty good."

"Sure," I say, even though I had no intention of attending any Plaza Live ever. But it seems I'm incapable of denying Sadie anything she asks of me. My pack will laugh their heads off if they find out. But there's no way I'm missing a chance to see Sadie again. Not because I"m going to try anything with her. Just to make sure she's safe from Bonehead. "I'll be there."

"Okay. Night, Deke." She's gazing at me, her face upturned.

Don't touch her. Don't touch her. Definitely don't kiss her.

I can't stop myself from reaching out, catching the back of her neck and drawing her close. Her vanilla scent washes over me, and I breathe it in like I just got out of prison, and this is my first breath of fresh air in a decade.

I muster some control and only press my lips to her forehead, where her hair's mussed and a bit damp from the helmet. I don't let myself taste her lips. And I don't get off the bike. If I dismount, there's no turning back.

After a moment, I let her go.

She backs up uncertainly, her pretty lips parted.

"Night, Sadie."

I don't ride off immediately. I wait until she's inside. She disappears, and the door lock clicks—my supernatural hearing won't let me miss a sound. What I don't hear is her moving away from the door, getting on with her night. The filmy white curtain in the window trembles a little, like she just twitched it aside. She's watching me.

I turn my bike back on and roll away. I still feel her silky skin under my lips. My wolf doesn't like me riding away. The instinct to turn the bike around and drive back nearly chokes me.

My wolf wants Sadie. He wants me to get her under me, tonight. He wants me to mark her as my own. Keep her.

But that's not possible. Because he's not fucking safe. Marking a human is dangerous under the best of conditions, and my wolf? He doesn't know restraint.

So I'll be staying the fuck away from Sadie Diaz. Because there's never been a human I needed to protect more.

Sadie

Despite the drinks and the night air, I'm not sleepy at all after Deke drops me off. I put the jackalope doll by the front door and flitter about my one-bedroom apartment organizing myself for the morning.

I'm all fluttery and excited. Also freaking out.

I've never done anything so reckless in my life. I *am* the type who is too trusting of strangers—I've been told that by my dad and my friends at least fifty-seven times. But I don't usually go around actively soliciting strange men. Or engaging in questionable activities like getting on the back of a motorcycle with one.

But my instincts told me he could be trusted.

And they were right! I was perfectly safe the whole time. I wore a helmet. He took me straight home when I asked him to, and he didn't even try anything with me—a fact I find myself slightly disappointed over. He wasn't the man-whore Charlie warned me of. He only kissed my forehead! Maybe he's not interested, and that's fine. I still loved every second of it.

Maybe I'm the adrenaline junkie because I'm all amped up now at my wild behavior. I have to say, it felt great to pretend I might date a guy like Deke. A big, bad, motorcycle-military guy. I let my wild out a little bit tonight. It felt rebellious and fun. I felt in charge of my own destiny for the first time in… I don't know how long.

Maybe since my mom left.

I flop back on my bed, and a puff of laughter comes from my lips.

When my phone buzzes with a text, I snatch it up. The twisted sick anticipation of finding another text from Scott is gone, replaced by anger.

This guy needs to leave me alone.

Sure enough, it's from Scott. *Sadie, I'm really worried about you. That guy you were with tonight is trouble.*

Instead of ignoring the text like I usually do, this time I answer. *Stop texting me. I don't ever want to hear from you again. It's over.*

There. I feel like I said that before, but I was being Sweet Sadie then. Now, I don't think I could be more clear.

Turns out standing up for myself feels good.

I roll onto my side, my thoughts slipping back to Deke. Of course, I wouldn't really date a guy like him. He wouldn't be interested in someone like me, for one thing.

And I doubt we have anything at all in common.

Still, the memory of his huge hand cupping my nape or the way he caged me in against the building in the alleyway—not like he was trapping me. More like he was shielding me—flit through my mind producing those butterflies in my belly.

What would it be like to run my hands over that chiseled body? To feel the power of his massive body over mine? Or under mine?

I slip my fingers between my legs and moan softly when they make contact. I pretend my fingers are Deke's giant ones. How would he touch me? Would he be rough? Or gentle?

Somehow I'm sure he'd be gentle. A big guy like him would've learned restraint with a woman. I bet he'd know exactly how to touch me. I'll bet he wouldn't critique my performance the way Scott used to.

Ugh. I don't want to think of Scott ever again.

Maybe he's what I need to move on. I'm sure he's not looking for a girlfriend. Especially not with someone like me. And we wouldn't work anyway—I mean, my dad would never accept a guy like him for me.

But maybe we could hook up. A wild fling to help me get back into the dating scene.

I roll over to my belly, my fingers still working between my legs. The idea has me all hot and bothered. I bite my pillow and wriggle my hips over my hand.

I'm not even embarrassed when I croak, "Deke!" into the bedcovers when I come.

CHAPTER 3

adie

I GO to the plaza early the next evening, before the music has even started. I stake out one of the tables and set down the plastic-covered platter of motorcycle-shaped sugar cookies I baked for Deke as a thank you. But I'm too nervous to sit. I stand behind the chair, shifting from foot to foot with my filmy skirt swirling around my legs. I'm all dressed up today in a yellow cotton sundress and stylish suede booties. As always, I brought my white cardigan in case it gets cold, but with the dress' deep v-neck and flirty hem, my outfit is on the risque side of "kindergarten teacher chic." Especially because I'm wearing the large hoop earrings Tabitha gave me. "Sexy and I know it" earrings, she calls them.

The band sets up, plugging things in and testing amps. One of the guitarists strums his electric bass, and the amp barks then squeals. A few rowdy tourists on the restaurant's patio holler back, but the crowd around the small stage and on the lawn starts to grow. People spread blankets out and open containers of food.

Deke isn't here yet, but I didn't think he'd get here early. I honestly don't know if he'll show up at all. Surely he has more important things to do than hang out in the plaza with me. I looked up Black Wolf Security online, but there's almost nothing about it. Their website is a black page with their wolf logo and nothing else. I bet Deke made it. It is so him.

The business license is registered to a PO Box in Taos. I'm tempted to ask Charlie to look into it, but then she'll know, and for now, I want to keep Deke my dirty little secret. Not that we've done anything dirty.

Unfortunately.

Yet.

When the music finally starts, I take a seat and check my phone. Scott did text me today but only twice. *Are you seriously seeing that guy?* he asked around midday. I waited until my bathroom break to text back my one word reply. "Yes." Technically, I am seeing Deke. Hopefully, he'll show up for the band like he said.

Scott's reply made my stomach clench. *What would your father say?* He always knew how to stick the knife in.

I tuck my phone away. Screw him. Screw them both. I don't want to think about what my father would say. Dad approved of Scott, no question. Whenever we went out to dinner together, always at the nicest restaurants in Taos, the two of them hogged the conversation, talking over me. I always suspected Scott dated me because my father's on the town council and well-connected. I didn't think it was the main reason, but looking back, I'm not so sure. Scott never seemed satisfied dating me. His cheating on me drove that home.

Is Deke the sort of guy who cheats? He's so hot, with epic levels of masculine bad-assery. I can't imagine him meeting a heterosexual woman who didn't swoon over him and offer up her panties in tribute.

But the way he looked at me, the intensity in his eyes...it made me feel like the only woman in the world.

I'm probably wrong. Deke's probably a player. But I'm willing to be another notch on his bedpost. That motorcycle ride is the most exciting thing that's happened to me in a long time. Maybe ever.

No—not happened to me.

I made it happen. I think that's half the excitement there.

The other half is definitely the extremely fit biker who drove it.

Up on stage, the band is rocking out. The sun is setting, and there's a good crowd for a Thursday night.

"Is this seat taken?" a woman asks me, her fingers already curling on the seat's back, ready to carry it away. She has long pink fingernails, tight jeans and a low cut black top. Why didn't I wear an outfit like that? She looks more like a biker babe than I ever will.

"Yes, it's taken," I tell her, jealousy making my voice sharp. She rolls her eyes, shaking her head as she struts away. I can almost hear her thoughts about me, but I don't care. It's nice to not be nice all the time.

"He'll show up," I whisper to myself. I'm sitting with my legs crossed primly at the ankle, my hands folded in my lap like a good little kindergarten teacher. My hair is tied back with a bow, for frick's sake.

I rise and tug off the bow, shaking out my hair. That's when I sense him. The hairs rise on the back of my neck, and the scent of motor oil and leather hits me.

I turn and scan the crowd but don't see Deke at first. But I know he's here.

And then he appears, stepping out of the shadows and striding towards me. There's a group of sexy snow bunny types standing in his path. They poke each other and stare at Deke, wide-eyed. But he doesn't even glance at them as he heads straight toward me. He's got that intense look again, the one that makes me shiver. I feel a little like I'm being hunted.

"Babe." He uses the word to convey whole sentences. I just have to decipher what they mean. He strolls right up to me. For a big guy, he moves with grace, prowling like a panther. He's wearing the same sort of outfit he wore before, dark jeans and a soft white t-shirt that clings to his abs. Big motorcycle boots.

My mouth waters.

He's so gosh darn hot. And I baked him cookies. What was I thinking?

"Deke. You came." I step in front of the table, hoping he won't see the cookie tray.

Of course, he spots it immediately. "What are these?" He reaches around me and touches the plastic.

"Um, just a little thank you. You know, for yesterday."

"You baked me cookies?"

"Yes."

"Babe," he says again and tucks a strand of hair behind my ear. "Thank you." He doesn't smile, but his dark gaze smolders. Up close, he's overwhelmingly sexy. My thighs clench, and I stifle a whimper.

"It's nothing." I turn away and fiddle with the plastic wrap around the cookie tray. "I owed you."

"Yeah?" He cocks his head to the side, still totally

focused on me. The young women still gawk at Deke, and he hasn't even noticed.

I swallow and step closer, so I don't have to shout over the music. "For last night. You're my hero."

His forehead creases. "I am not a hero."

I want to argue, but I realize I would sound foolish. I obviously made last night into a bigger deal than it is to him.

"Well, I still owe you." I summon my bravery and put my hand on his chest.

He raises a dark brow. "Oh yeah? You owe me?" There's a suggestive purr to his voice.

Heat shoots between my legs. "If you ever need me to be your fake girlfriend, let me know," I say, half joking. As if he couldn't snap his fingers and get any sort of woman to do anything he wanted.

"Babe." He hits me with that intense stare of his—so hot it could burn off all my clothes. His lips twitch like he thinks I'm cute. Then he leans close and whispers, "With me, you wouldn't be faking anything." His voice is deep and rich with the pure promise of sex.

I flush. Goosebumps break out all over my body.

The song the band is playing abruptly ends. The crowd sends up a half-hearted cheer. Deke straightens, and I take in his expression. He looks dead serious now.

I turn and clap for the band, but I can feel Deke still focused on me.

"Thank you," the lead guitarist shouts into the microphone. "We're the Flying Oysters. This is for all the lovebirds out there."

And they start playing "Undisclosed Desires" by Muse. One of my favorite songs. Not a typical love song although I think it's sexy.

I lick my lips, and Deke's gaze drops to my mouth. "I

love this song," I tell him. He nods slowly. His eyes glitter green in the low light, flashing like a cat's. I lean forward to ask him about it when he takes my hand and abruptly leads me away from the table.

I follow without question, every nerve on fire. He pulls me along behind him, away from the crowd, out of the plaza, into an alleyway full of shadows. It's dark and private, and I have no idea what's going on, but just like last night, none of my stranger danger alarms go off. I'm relaxed, content to be with him.

"What are we doing here?"

He turns, his big body herding me backwards until I'm caged between him and the wall.

"Deke?" I ask, suddenly breathless.

"I'm collecting that favor." His nose is close enough to touch mine.

A thrum begins between my legs.

With a growl, he pins my hips with his. He leans his forearm on the wall above my head, his huge biceps blocking out all light. His right hand cups my cheek. I open my mouth, and his face descends.

He kisses me right there in the alley. My toes curl in my boots. The wall at my back is cold, but the heat from Deke's body warms me through and through.

He groans and pulls his head back but keeps me pinned, his eyes flashing weirdly in the dark. "This is what I want—your kiss. This is all I want." He kisses me again.

I surge up against him, grabbing handfuls of his soft t-shirt as if I could pull him into my body. He angles his head, and his tongue slips into my mouth. I moan.

He tears his mouth from mine and backs away, his chest heaving. The place between my legs is liquid, aching. I lean against the adobe brick wall, gasping. I was seconds away from coming from his tongue fucking my mouth.

"Deke," I whisper.

"Sadie." He touches my lip with a finger. When he drops his hand I realize he's shaking.

He steps away, half turning. "I'm sorry." His voice is hoarse and deep. "I shouldn't do this."

"No, you should." I blurt. "You very much should." I would raise my skirt for him right here in the alley.

"Fuck." He runs a hand over his head. He's about to say something else, when the roar of a motorcycle cuts through the air.

"Fuck," Deke shouts, and he steps away as a man on a bike appears at the mouth of the alley. Deke's big body blocks most of my view. I don't know what's happening.

The big biker is wearing one of those skull cap type helmets that doesn't cover your face or offer any real protection. His face looks familiar, like he might be one of the bikers with Deke yesterday, but I can't be sure. He's got blond hair, and his eyes flash in the dark like Deke's do. "I thought I'd find you here," he says to Deke.

"What the fuck do you want?" Deke growls back.

"Rafe wants to see you."

Deke swears some more.

"What's going on?" I ask, and Deke spins to face me. His shoulders are tense, and he somehow looks bigger than before.

"I shouldn't have done this," he tells me, and my heart plummets to my feet.

"What?" I whisper.

"Sadie." His tone is pleading. "I'm sorry. I should've stayed away."

What the heck?

"Deke," his friend calls, and Deke wrenches backwards like he's being tugged with a rope. His face is pained. I don't like it.

"Excuse me." I march out of the alleyway. My cardigan is askew, and my hair is all tousled from the crazy kiss fest, but I don't care. "What's going on?" I use my stern-teacher voice with the blond biker.

The guy grins. "This is who you've been sniffing around?" he says to Deke. "She's cute for a civilian. I like her."

My head explodes. "I beg your pardon?" I growl. The sound is as impressive as Deke's, if I do say so myself. "Who the heck are you?"

The blond grins wider.

"Sadie," Deke steps between me and the biker. "I have to go."

"Why?"

He shrugs, but he looks unhappy. "We're not supposed to mix with civilians. But call me if you need help again. Anytime at all."

"Deke," his friend warns, but this time Deke ignores him.

"Promise me," Deke says quietly to me.

"I promise," I whisper back. Before I can step forward and hug him, he whirls and strides away. His friend remains on his bike, blocking me from following. I glare, but it doesn't seem to bother him. After a minute, he gives me a mock mini salute and rides away.

I stand at the mouth of the cold dark alley, staring down the empty road.

What the heck just happened?

Deke

I RIDE with Lance until we get to the mountain road that leads to the pack's land. Then I gun my hog past the entrance. I'm not following him home like some little lost puppy.

I know my Alpha sent Lance to watch over me. I'm even okay with it. I have no business messing around with a civilian, especially one like Sadie. She's outta my league in every way. Thinking about it makes me want to howl.

My bike speeds up the switchbacks. I take each turn faster and faster, imagining Sadie pressed into my back. My cock perks up, and I grit my teeth.

I pull off the road onto an overlook. Out here, the city lights mirror the carpet of stars above. I'd like to show Sadie this.

The peaceful quiet is shattered by a motorcycle zooming past. I stiffen then strip off my vest. I kick off my boots and shuck my jeans. I'm left in my white shirt, and I step behind my bike to hide my nudity.

The motorcycle comes roaring back down the road. It slows when it reaches the overlook and glides to a stop a few feet away. The rider pulls off his helmet.

It's Channing. I knew it was him. He's the only one of us who rides a neon green bike and not a real hog. He's such a tool on his stupid crotch rocket.

"Deke, what the fuck? You know you can't get too close to a human—"

I don't give him any warning. I leap into the air and let my wolf rip out of me. The t-shirt shreds, tearing painfully on my twisted limbs. But I was always quick to shift.

By the time Channing knows what's going on, I've leapt over my bike. He scrambles off his bike a second before two hundred plus pounds of black wolf hits him in the chest. We both go down—him and his crotch rocket, and me on him. He swipes at me, his hands changed to massive paws, but I jump off him and dance away.

"Fuck," he shouts. "Motherfucker." He rises, struggling to get free of his clothes. He sees his bike lying on its side, the shiny paint scratched on the road, and he gets even more stupid with rage. "You're going to fucking pay for that." His claws tear at his clothes. Stupid fucker's gonna have to ride home naked. He'll take it out of my hide. I had the element of surprise, but once he's in wolf form, we're pretty evenly matched. When he's riled up, like now, he can tear me up.

Good.

A growl splits the air, and a giant white and brown wolf stalks stiff legged towards me. Channing the wolf lowers his belly almost to the ground, his ears back and teeth bared, ready to pounce.

I grin like a maniac and brace myself, waiting for pain.

Sadie

When I'm back in my apartment, I set down the untouched platter of cookies on the table and check my phone. I've got missed calls from Adele, Charlie and Tabitha. I sigh and dial Adele.

"Sadie!" She answers on the first ring. "Thank God. Are you home?"

"Yes." I toss my keys onto my countertop. "Is everything okay?"

"We're coming over. Be there in fifteen." She hangs up.

Well, shoot. I hurry to put a few dirty dishes away in my sink and wipe a few coffee stains off my counter. Then I open a bottle of red wine, a blend Adele bought for me. After tonight, I need a glass of wine.

Who was that guy on the motorcycle? He was one of Deke's friends, but he didn't act like it. He totally cock-blocked Deke. And me.

What's the lady equivalent of cockblocking? Muffin Muzzle? Beaver Damned? Clit-erference? I'll ask Tabitha, she'd know. Whatever the female equivalent of cockblocking, that dude Deke knew did it to me.

Did I really want to have sex up against a wall with Deke in a dark alley way?

Yes, my ovaries shout. *Yes, we want his surly biker babies!*

My ovaries were never so vocal when Scott was around, and Scott, by outward appearances, would have made a far more respectable father of my children. It's so weird. I never would've said that tough-looking biker was my thing.

Never in a million years.

I slosh wine into a glass and take a gulp.

Adele knocks on the door, and when I open it, I realize who she meant by *we.* Adele tromps in, followed by Tabitha and Charlie.

"Oh, hello, everyone," I say. "I have wine."

"We brought extra," Adele says. Both Charlie and Tabitha lift the bottles they're holding. Adele heads straight for my small kitchen and makes herself at home, grabbing three more glasses and pouring wine for all. I let her take over—Adele's a chef, so my kitchen is in good hands—and head to my cozy living room.

"You doing okay?" Tabitha trails me, and we both settle on the couch.

"Of course," I answer noncommittally although my voice is noticeably subdued. I haven't even asked why they all dropped everything to come over. I think I already know.

Charlie drops into her usual seat—a bean bag chair I keep next to the fireplace. Both she and Tabitha look at me expectantly. I knew they'd figure out something was up with me and Deke; it was only a matter of time. It's a small town, and word travels at lightning speed. If anyone saw us in the alley tonight, the news would get back to my friends immediately.

Instead of asking who saw what, I turn to Tabitha. "What's the female equivalent of cockblocking?"

"*Clam-jam*," Tabitha replies immediately. I knew she'd know.

"I prefer *Pussy Putt*," Charlie says.

"That doesn't make any sense," Tabitha retorts.

"Twat Blocker," Charlie offers, and she and Tabitha start arguing about sports metaphors involving vaginas.

"Okay, that's enough," Adele strides into the living room. She doesn't sit but stands with her back to the kiva fireplace holding her wine, looking down imperiously at all of us before her focus sharpens on me. "Sadie, do you have something to share with the class?"

I sigh. "Who spotted me?"

"I did," Tabitha raises her hand sheepishly. "And I was worried, so I told everyone."

"What exactly did you see?"

"You with the big bad biker at the plaza tonight," Tabitha says. "I was going to come over, but after I was done texting everyone, I looked up and you'd disappeared."

Adele searches my face, looking concerned, "You know we were joking about you hooking up with a biker, right?"

I shrug. "I don't know, I kind of thought the idea had its merits."

All three of my friends stare at me in shock.

"He's actually quite sweet."

"Sweet?" Charlie repeats dubiously.

I hasten to explain. "Last night, Scott tried to ambush me, so I asked Deke to help me out and pretend to be my date. And he did. He's really nice."

"Hold on. Back up," Adele says. "Scott tried to ambush you?"

"Yeah. I guess he installed a tracking app on my phone, so he knew I was in the plaza. And then he knew I'd get a rideshare home because it was Whine Wednesday, so he parked himself at the rideshare stop, so we could talk."

"My goodness. He's gone from delusional to full blown stalker," Adele says.

"I'll kill him," Tabitha mutters.

"I'll help," Charlie says.

"But it's all good. Deke helped me, and Scott backed off."

"How did Deke help? Did he threaten Scott?"

"Not really." I think back on those beautiful moments when I had the big biker beside me, silent and strong. The best kind of backup. "He had my back while I made myself clear to Scott. Then he reaffirmed what I said, invited me on his bike, and we rode off together." I can't stop the stupid grin from stretching across my face. It's the only crazy thing I've ever done in my life, and I'm quite proud of it.

"You did what?!" My friends explode as one.

"I can't believe you rode off with him," Tabitha gasps.

"Did you let anyone know where you were?" Adele asks. "Take a photo of his license plate? Anything?"

"You got on his bike? So cool!" Charlie says.

"No, not cool," Tabitha frowns at Charlie. "She got on a strange man's bike. He could've motored to the middle of nowhere, and we'd never hear from Sadie again!"

"Yeah, but she'd get to ride that awesome motorcycle first," Charlie points out with her tongue firmly in cheek and then ducks when Tabitha mimes throwing a pillow at her head.

"Calm down. Nothing bad happened," Adele raises her hands in an effort to keep the peace. "Right, Sadie?"

"I was fine. He was a perfect gentleman." I blush, remembering that ride. My body pressed against Deke's giant body, the bike rumbling between my legs. "I know it's not something I'd normally do, but I felt totally safe with him," I add softly.

My friends are quiet, processing this.

"So what happened tonight?" Tabitha asks.

I shrug. "I invited him to meet me. I made him cookies as a thank you. And..."

"And?" Adele and the other two lean in closer.

"And...he took me to the alleyway and kissed me."

Another explosion.

"I knew it." Tabitha punches the pillow she's holding.

"Nice." Charlie sags back into her bean bag chair. "Was it good?"

"Look at her blush. Of course, it was good," Tabitha says.

Adele grabs her wine glass and takes a long swallow, watching me over the rim.

"Did you use protection?" Tabitha jokes, wagging a finger at me.

My cheeks are an inferno. "It didn't get that far."

"But it would have?" Charlie's eyes grow wide.

"It was a really, really good kiss." I fold my hands in my lap, doing my best prim teacher impression. "That's all I'm going to say."

"You okay?" Adele asks. Her green eyes probe me.

"I'm good. After the kiss, he had to go."

"I'll bet twenty bucks Scott finds out and shows up again at Sadie's school with flowers," Charlie announces to the room.

"That is so rude. We shouldn't be betting on Sadie's love life," Tabitha shakes her head at Charlie. "But I'll take that bet."

Charlie just grins.

"What I want to know is if you're seeing him again," Adele says.

My giddy feelings drop away. "I don't know. He left pretty abruptly. One of his biker buddies rode up and said he had to go. It was kind of weird."

"That was the clam-jam?" Tabitha asks.

I nod.

"Sadie, maybe it's for the best." Adele doesn't make eye contact with me. She's focused on her wine glass, moving it gently so the garnet liquid swirls.

"What do you mean by that?" Tabitha asks.

Adele bites her lip then says, "I did some digging. These guys are military. Like, special ops. Top secret missions and all that. Probably American assassins."

"What branch of the military?" Charlie asks.

"Army. Special forces. They were honorably discharged last year."

I cock my head to the side. "How do you know all this?"

Adele raises one slim shoulder in a half shrug. She still doesn't look at me.

"Adele works in mysterious ways," Tabitha says into the awkward silence.

"Well, now they're like a motorcycle gang or something," Charlie offers. "They bought an old ski valley resort and use it as their home base."

"They're called clubs not gangs," Adele corrects.

"So they're in a club." Tabitha stretches out her long legs, slouching further into my couch. "So what? That's not a crime."

"There's more than that," Adele sighs. "Deke has a record. Assault and battery. He lost it in a bar and beat a guy up. Put him in the hospital. The cops investigated, but the guy didn't end up pressing charges."

There's a silence while we all absorb this.

"I see," I say. "Is that why you staged this little intervention?"

"She called us up and told us you'd been spotted with the biker dude. We couldn't stay away," Tabitha said.

"We care about you, Sadie," Charlie says.

I can't sit any longer. "Deke's not like that." I cross to the kitchen and grab my cardigan, tugging it on and rubbing my arms like I'm cold. "He wouldn't hurt me." I think it through. "If that happened, he was probably protecting a woman. He's that kind of guy."

My friends watch me from the living room. They don't say anything, but I can hear the unspoken question. *How do you know?*

How do I know? It's just a feeling. But then I'm not that great a judge of people. I was with Scott, after all.

"I'm not saying he's not a bad person." I realize I'm pacing and halt. "I don't know him that well, but I feel safe with him." I run a hand through my hair. It's still tangled. I can still feel his big hands on me, his breath on my face. I relive the kiss and arousal shoots from the pit of my belly and blossoms between my legs.

"I didn't say that," Adele hesitates, her normal poise broken as she chooses her words. She looks really worried. "I just think you should be careful. We don't want you to get hurt."

This is ridiculous. First, Deke's biker friend and now my friends. Are my instincts about him wrong?

I'm sorry. He told me. *I should've stayed away.* Is he really so dangerous?

"Well, don't worry about me," I say with a fake laugh. "I doubt I'll ever see Deke again."

"I'm sorry," Tabitha says, sounding subdued. "It sounds like that might be for the best."

~

Deke

AFTER THE FIGHT, Channing's wolf pants on the side of the road, blood slicking his fur, staining the white patches red. With a silent snarl, he slinks into the brush, heading off to lick his wounds and shift.

The rage inside me still burns. My wolf walks stiff legged back to my bike. Scraps of white fabric litter the ground. My t-shirt. The one Sadie dug her hands into when I kissed her. The fabric still bears her scent.

I point my nose to the moon and howl.

After I shift, I ride for an extra hour, up and down Taos Mountain until my hands are stiff on the handlebars. Then I turn and head down the dark road home.

The pack bought a mountain lodge sometime back. We always knew we'd need to retire someplace remote where we can run free as wolves. Last year, Rafe decided it was time to get out of the service. It wasn't that our missions were getting harder and more dangerous—although they were. We were a unit, a secret regiment of shifters united under a colonel who knew what we were. When we were on a mission, we thrived.

We flew in under the cover of night, our super senses making it easy for us to see when humans couldn't. We did the blackest of black ops, and we loved every moment. We loved it too much.

Rafe could tell we were losing our humanity. Especially me. He decided our wolves required more space and freedom for the safety of everyone around us. The Colonel agreed and had reasons to want us as private contractors, instead. He arranged an honorable discharge with healthy retirement packages then hired us for the same type of missions we were doing before, only now the government could claim no knowledge of us if things went wrong. A privilege they are willing to pay handsomely for.

But for me and my wolf, it was too late. My wolf loves the thrill of the kill and always would. Even now, a year into retirement, my wolf is savage. Broken. Rafe tried to save me, I'm already too far gone.

I ride my bike right into the giant hangar we use as a garage. When I turn the engine off, the silence assaults my ears. I prefer the noise and vibration of the motorcycle—the riot calms the demons inside me.

"Deke." My alpha steps out from behind the Humvee. He's not fooling anyone—I scented him as soon as I rode up.

"Alpha," I say. A growl tinges my voice without me meaning it too. My wolf is amped up, ready to fight. Like always.

"You smell like that human," Rafe says.

I grunt and pick up a clean cloth hanging from a hook on the wall by the tool rack. I swipe it over my leather seat, pretending to clean off a bit of mud.

"You think I didn't scent her on you last night?" Rafe jerks his nose into the air and sniffs. "Civilian. Sadie Diaz. Kindergarten teacher. Her ancestors were original Spanish settlers in the area. Father's on the city council. Scott Sears is her ex."

A growl rumbles in my chest. "You looked into her."

"Course I did. I haven't seen you so interested in a human before."

"It's nothing," I lie. Which is stupid because any shifter can tell when someone's lying. I toss the cloth away. "I'll probably never see her again." My wolf snarls at the thought.

"You *won't* see her again," my alpha says firmly.

Fuck this. I snarl again, this time out loud, and stomp out of the hangar.

"You can't claim her, Deke," Rafe calls after me. "You don't know what your wolf will do."

He's right. My wolf is a monster, out of control. The only thing I'm good at is killing. And one day, I'll go too far, and my pack will have to put me down.

I can't see Sadie again.

It's for the best.

CHAPTER 4

Sadie

THIS MORNING my eyes are gritty, and I'm exhausted. If my kids or fellow teachers notice my smile is a bit forced, they don't say anything.

I didn't cry over Deke. I barely defended him to my friends. They left after I gave them a half-hearted promise to let them know if Scott makes another move.

I don't care about Scott. My thoughts are consumed by the big biker and our supernova kiss. I barely knew Deke, and my heart feels empty, like he already made a place for himself, and now he's gone.

I bring the motorcycle cookies to my classroom. Charlie stole two last night, but there are still plenty.

We're out for recess when one of my students tugs on my skirt. "Miss Sadie, there's a man here to see you."

Sure enough, there's Scott in navy slacks and a tie with a bouquet of red roses crossing the parking lot towards our enclosed playground. My lip curls. Roses? So cliché. I pull out my phone to text Charlie that she won the bet.

I signal to my fellow teachers that I'm going to go deal with this and march to the gate. Scott smiles when he sees me. I can practically see him flip a switch to "charming." His thinning hair blows in the breeze. No amount of fancy product can hide the fact that he'll eventually go bald. It's petty of me to look forward to it, but if Scott cared half as much for being a decent person as he does his grooming, he'd might be tolerable to be around maybe.

Why did I ever date him? Was I really that desperate for my dad's approval?

"Scott." I cross my arms over my chest. "What are you doing here?"

"Council meeting next door. But I knew I would see you." He proffers the flowers. I raise a brow.

"I can't accept these. We're not together any more." Darn him for putting me in this position in front of my students.

The smile slips a little from Scott's face. "Why not? Sadie, we were good together."

I can't help it. I half laugh. It's so far from the truth, it's funny. Amazing I never saw it that way before.

Scott's smile is gone now, and I catch a glimpse of something else, something ugly. "You're not acting like yourself, Sadie. You're not usually like this."

"Maybe this is who I am. Maybe before I was too nice. I deserve to have you respect my boundaries."

"Is it that biker? His influence? Are you really seeing him?" He shakes his head. "Your dad is going to flip."

I'm about to answer when the roar of motorcycles interrupts. Two Harley Davidsons roll up to the parking lot next door. The huge bikers pilot their bikes into a shared parking space, then dismount. The sunlight glints off their aviator shades. They're in dark jeans that hug their powerful thighs and black leather jackets. They look like they just walked off the set of the most badass action movie ever filmed.

As they get closer, I recognize them. Deke and one of the other guys from the plaza two nights ago. A flush rolls up from my toes, heat climbing steadily towards my cheeks. My heartbeat thuds in my ears.

I'm not the only one who notices the bikers. Half my class is pressed against the fence, pointing to the motorcycles.

"So cool," one little girl shouts. "Miss Sadie, those are motorcycles. Like the cookies you brought us."

A breeze kicks up, and Deke's head snaps my way. I give a little wave and lean back on the fence to compensate for my suddenly weak knees. Deke immediately alters his course to detour away from the school entrance to where I stand. After a second's hesitation, so does his biker buddy.

Deke arrives first, his shades pointed right at me. "Sadie."

"Deke," I greet him, my voice catching a little. He looks good. Behind him, his buddy scowls at me. It's not the blond from last night but a different guy who clears his throat as if he doesn't want Deke to forget he's there.

Deke steps to the side and jerks his head to his buddy. "This is Rafe."

"Hi, Rafe," I say. We're all standing in a loose circle, me with my back to the fence, Scott to my left, Deke right in front of me, and his buddy at his left elbow. Not awkward at all.

Scott clears his throat, annoyed at being left out. "Excuse us," he says, and his voice is high and whiny compared to Deke's deep rumble.

"Sears," Deke says, with a brief glance at the flowers Scott brought.

"Adalwulf." Scott tries to face off with Deke, but Deke refuses to look at him.

"What are you guys doing here?" I ask both Deke and Rafe.

"Council meeting. City's hiring us for some security," Rafe answers. Deke just looks at me. I can't see his eyes behind his shades, but my insides quiver like I'm stripped naked.

Nope, did not imagine the intensity between us. And it isn't going away. It's getting stronger.

"Cookies?" asks Deke, raising a brow.

"You heard that?" I am full on blushing now.

"You gave mine away."

"You left without taking them."

This time both Rafe and Scott clear their throats, and I realize Deke and I are talking like it's only the two of us.

"So you guys do security?" I ask Rafe.

"We do. We're former military."

"Rafe was my staff sergeant," Deke says.

A small hand tugs the edge of my sweater. "Miss Sadie, can they come next week?" Jenny, one of my kindergarteners, asks.

I smile down at her and the little boys who are gathered at the fence. "I don't know, Mr. Rafe and Mr. Deke are very busy. Do you want me to ask them?"

A chorus of excited yeses rises up from the kids. A few jump up and down.

"What's next week?" Scott asks. I ignore him and say to Rafe, "We do a career day every Tuesday. We had the fire department last week. Could you guys come and talk about your service?"

The corner of Rafe's mouth quirks up as if he's amused by something, but all he says is, "Sure. Here." He hands me a white business card. "My email and cell are on that. Call anytime, and we'll set it up."

"Will do." I nod to him coolly. I'm still miffed about the no mixing with civilians rule that made Deke's biker friend interrupt our moment last night.

"Sadie," Scott says, but the bell rings.

"Got to go. I can't take those," I tell Scott, waving a hand at the rose bouquet. "One of my students is allergic." I turn my back on him and smile up at Deke. "See you next week. Rafe, nice to meet you."

The back of my neck tingles as I walk away. I stand against the wall by the door, and my kids fall into line. I know Deke's watching, and it puts a big smile on my face. Fate brought us together today, and if everything goes well, next week, I'll get to see him again. I already can't wait.

Deke

"Gotta admit," Rafe says as we watch Sadie guide her students back toward the school, "Your little human's got a backbone."

"She's not mine," I mutter. "Per your orders, as I recall." My wolf howls at my denial. I don't bother giving Sears a second glance before heading off to the school entrance.

Rafe falls into step beside me. "Once you saw Sears with her, you couldn't get over there fast enough. Is he bothering her?"

"Yep." I don't say anything else, but Rafe can probably hear my teeth grinding.

"You didn't punch him in the face. Pretty impressive restraint."

"Yeah, I should win a prize." I rub a hand over my face. Seeing Sears with Sadie made me want to shove the guy's head in his trunk and slam the door down on him. Repeatedly. And then throw her over my shoulder and carry her back to my place, caveman style. For protection.

And orgasms. I want to give Sadie Diaz all the orgasms. Enough pleasure to make her forget that guy ever was in her life.

"You wouldn't really visit her classroom, would you?"

Rafe shrugs. "Why not? It's community service. We have to give something back to Taos."

"Do you think that's smart?"

Rafe turns to me. He tilts his head. To his credit, he takes the question seriously. "What do you think, soldier? You think your wolf can behave around a bunch of five and six-year-olds?"

I swallow. I think I can keep my wolf reined in but don't want to promise anything. "Probably shouldn't risk it."

"Objection noted. But if we go, you're coming with us. I won't let your wolf get out of line. And I think it'd be good for you."

I nod, shocked.

Then my alpha points a finger in my face. "But stay away from Sadie Diaz. That's an order."

My wolf growls, and I stifle it before the sound can rumble out of my chest. "Yes, sir," I say stiffly.

"It's the right thing to do, Deke. Humans aren't for us." He searches my eyes before nodding and walking away. I follow more slowly.

Humans aren't for us.

I could argue with him. There are a few wolf shifters we

know who have mated humans. Not that I'd ever call them up and ask them how it works. It doesn't matter, not in my case.

I'm too feral to ever be trusted with a human female. Especially not one as gentle as Sadie.

Sadie

As soon as I'm home, I take out Rafe's card. *Black Wolf Security.* It lists his name, Rafe Lightfoot. There are two numbers, office and cell. After a second of hesitation, I call the office. A recorded woman's voice invites me to leave a message, so I leave my name and number and the details of the career day.

A minute later my phone vibrates with a text. "This is Deke."

I grab my phone and clutch it to my heart. This is exactly what I hoped would happen when I left a message on the office phone instead of calling Rafe directly. I know Deke gave me his number, but after the way we left things last time, I wasn't sure if he wanted to hear from me.

"How did you get this number?" I type out and send before I get nervous and delete it.

No answer.

"Just kidding. I was teasing. I'm glad you texted," I type quickly.

Still no answer.

And then my phone rings. I fumble with it and almost drop it before I answer.

"Hello?" My voice is breathless like I've just run a marathon and then up a flight of stairs. Which is exactly what

I'll tell Deke if he asks why I'm out of breath—that I just got back from a run.

"Babe," he drawls, low and deep, and I feel it in the pit of my belly.

"Hey," I say with a smile in my voice and collapse slowly backwards onto my bed. "You got my message." I'm too excited to tease him about it.

"Happened to be in the office."

"I hoped you'd get it."

He makes a low rumbling sound. A chuckle? I can't tell. I bite my lip before I blurt out that I've selected him for my rebound fling. So much for playing my feelings close to the chest.

"Thought you were calling Rafe about a career day not me," he chides gently.

"I was. But maybe I wanted you to get my number." My insides scrunch with my boldness. It's not like me. It's like I'm braver around Deke. Or my feelings are too strong to hold in.

After a pause, he says in a rougher voice, "I already got your number. The night I gave you a ride."

"Oh right, you're one of those tech guys who can figure everything out." It's my turn to chide. "Why didn't you call me?"

"You didn't give me your number directly. And you've already got a stalker."

"You're not a stalker," I say quickly. I don't like the dark, almost painful tinge to his voice. "So, I get the feeling your biker peeps don't like me."

"What?" Deke asks after a pause.

"Your peeps. Friends or posse or whatever." I dance around calling them a *gang*. They seem tighter knit than friends, more like family. Brothers. I remember what Charlie said about them being in the service together.

"Why do you think they don't like you?"

I squint at my ceiling fan, thinking back over the last two meetings with Deke's buddies. One case of clam-jam, one of *flirtus interruptus.* "They seem to have a problem with me."

"It's not you they have a problem with." Deke clears his throat. "We're not supposed to mix with civilians, that's all."

"Why not? You're not even in the military any more, right?"

"We're still in a dangerous business. We go out on missions a lot. Dating isn't really allowed."

"How about casual hook-ups?" I blurt.

Deke coughs, like I just made him choke.

I twitch my inner thighs together, trying to alleviate the needy pulse between my legs.

"You know. If you wanted to collect that favor."

Silence.

Deke's quiet so long I wonder if he's still there. "Deke?"

"Sadie, it's not a good idea." His voice is rough, and I realize he sounds sad.

"Because you have a record?" I ask as gently as I can.

Another pause. "How did you find out about that?"

"I have my ways." I want to joke about being a badass super spy, but it sticks in my throat.

"Yeah. I'm dangerous."

"You were special ops. Of course, you're dangerous. Kinda the job description." I try to sound playful, but he's getting more distant. I'm losing him. I barely know him, and it already hurts.

I swallow, and it feels like there are knives lining my throat. "Can I at least call you?" I ask.

"Yeah, Sadie. You can call me."

CHAPTER 5

SWISS ALPS, FOUR DAYS LATER

*eke*

THE WIND WHIPS over the rocks and cleaves a path through our camp. The frozen breeze slices through my thin jacket. If I were human, I'd be shivering, but my shifter blood keeps me warm. Snow crunches under my boots as I make my way to Sierra One, the highest sniper position in our mission. Lance is already there on his belly, peering through his rifle scope down at the fancy ass chalet. We're deep in the Swiss Alps, high above our target.

My radio crackles, and Rafe's voice says, "Sierra One, this is TOC. You got eyes on Tango?"

"TOC, this is Sierra One," I respond. "No movement yet." Several hundred yards below our stakeout perch, the mansion is lit up like a candle, each window emanating a soft warm glow. Nestled in the side of the mountain, surrounded by snow-dusted pines, the castle looks like it's part of a Christmas village set. One of those kitschy toy ones grandmas put out around the holidays, with mounds of cotton balls to make fake snow. Except this place is real. Twenty-five thousand square feet of luxury housing, inhabited by the most successful black market arms dealer in the world. Gabriel Dieter, a guy who makes a living being pure evil.

"Should we move in closer?" Lance asks me softly, his eyes still trained on the target.

"We'd better not." The mission is surveillance only. Getting close could cause us to engage when we're just here to watch.

Of course, my wolf hates that. Just being on a mission brings on blood lust. My wolf wants to tear down the mountains, howling, take on the mansion security—guards, dogs, lasers—find Dieter and rip the Tango's head off. Mission accomplished. Which is why my alpha's concerned I'm not stable and sane.

"Movement, front left. Near the pool," Lance reports.

I lift the radio to my mouth. "TOC, we have movement. Eyes on Tango." I report the subject's movements. Gabriel Dieter is set to meet with a contingent from an unknown terrorist force. We're here to spy on the meeting, record Gabriel's movements and get any evidence we can of his illegal arms deals.

But first it looks like the man's going to use his fancy schmancy outdoor pool. Dieter walks out of the glass conservatory. He's a tall man, fit. A head full of dark hair with no sign of going grey or his body going to seed. Of course, anyone would be fit and toned if they had enough money to hire an army of cosmetic surgeons. Evil pays.

"Deke," Lance calls, and I realize my chest is rumbling with a growl. My wolf wants off the chain. I slide my hand into my pocket and touch my phone. It's become a habit, and it all started with Sadie's call a week ago.

She's taken to texting me every other day. A smiley emoji, a joke. "Happy Monday," she sent an hour ago, along with a picture of a cheerfully smiling sun. "Hope you have a great week." I shake my head at her optimism.

Reading her texts helps focus me. Just swiping a thumb over the smooth phone screen is enough to instantly calm my wolf.

I gotta get a grip. What would Sadie think about the things my wolf has done? What he wants to do? That thought sobers me.

"Movement in the house. Far right wing. Base of the turret."

I grab a pair of binoculars and check out the side of the mansion Lance is referring to. A door opens and black clad men are pouring out, each armed with tactical gear. Boots, knee pads, helmets and balaclava masks over their faces. And giant guns.

"Fuck." I swivel and get eyes on Gabriel Dieter again. The business mogul stands beside the pool, water dripping off his muscled chest. He raises a hand and waves right at me.

"Bastard." I toss the binoculars in the bag. "He knows we're here. Move out."

Lance is already on his feet. He has his rifle, I have our bags. We turn and race up the mountain.

The radio squawks. "We've been made," I holler into it.

Three hundred yards below us, men stream in coordinated lines up the mountains towards us.

"Abort mission. Get to high ground," Rafe orders.

Barking fills the air.

"They got dogs," Lance announces the obvious, and picks up his pace. We pound over the ice slick rocks, climbing the mountain peak. The air is thin, and my lungs burn, struggling to adapt. My legs scream for more energy while my head gets light.

"Come on, Deke," Lance calls. "Race you to the summit."

I push myself to climb faster. The snarls of the guard's dogs echo around us. They're getting closer. I hope our alpha's planned a surprise exit; otherwise, I don't know how this ends well.

My boots skid on black ice, and I halt, considering. I should stand my ground, give Lance a chance to escape. This is the way I could go out a hero. No one but my packmates would mourn my death.

And Sadie…

"Deke, what the fuck are you doing?" Lance skids to a halt a few yards ahead. Behind us the shouts and scrape of the militia's boots and barks of the dogs grow closer.

But there's another sound, this one up ahead. A *thuk-thuk-thuk* of helicopter blades.

Lance's face splits into a grin. "Sonofabitch," he murmurs. "He's done it again." We both turn and race up the mountain, headed for the snowy ridge as the bird appears, hovering over the summit.

"Heard you needed a ride," the pilot shouts over the din of the helicopter blades.

Rafe sticks his head out of the side and throws down a ladder. "Get the hell up here."

Lance leaps on the ladder and starts climbing. The militia chasing us shouts, and I grab the bottom of the ladder. Any second now, they'll start shooting. It's a miracle they haven't started already. Guess Dieter didn't think to ready any long range guns.

A few heartbeats later, Rafe and Channing haul me into the chopper, and the pilot spirits us away.

"What the fuck happened?" Rafe asks.

"He had eyes on us," I tell him. "He knew we were there."

Rafe curses. "I can't believe this."

"Is there a leak on our end?" Lance asks.

"No one knew about this except Colonel Johnson and our team. Dieter knew we were going to be there. Somehow, he knew." I can hear Rafe's teeth grinding.

Rafe growls and pulls out his phone. As soon as he's in range, he'll report to Colonel Johnson: Mission Aborted. We failed, but we'll live to try again another day.

When we're back at HQ, I pull up my phone and check to see if Sadie's texted me. I don't even have a picture of her, only her name and number saved in my Contacts folder, but seeing her name makes me scent her candy sweetness.

"Deke's texting his girlfriend," Lance singsongs.

I bare my teeth at him, and he chuckles and elbows Channing. "I'll bet you twenty bucks says he has her under him by full moon."

I don't think, I don't pause. Red washes over my vision, and the next thing I know, I'm on top of Lance. He's on the floor, and I'm pounding him with my fists.

"What the fuck," Channing shouts and tackles me, dragging me off of Lance. Lance's pretty face is bruised and bleeding, but the fucker is laughing hysterically. I push Channing away and retreat to the corner, trying to get my wolf under control.

"Settle down," Rafe orders as if we're kids roughhousing on a playground instead of three fully grown werewolves trying to kill each other.

"Well, you can't say this wasn't fun," Lance grins at me, his teeth streaked red. He's as crazy as I am, he just hides it better.

"Plane's almost here. Get cleaned up, so we can go," Rafe orders.

"Any other missions?" Channing asks Rafe.

"Nope. Next few weeks are quiet. Two security gigs and some surveillance. Oh," Rafe shoots a glance in my direction, "and visiting Sadie Diaz's kindergarten class."

My heart thumps when I hear her name. My wolf gets agitated in a new way. A far more frisky way.

Once I'm on the plane and strapped in, I reach into my pocket and find my phone. I swipe my thumb across the surface, touching it like a talisman.

The aftermath of battle has always been hard on my wolf. I've been honed into a killing machine, and it's difficult to come back to civilian life. The bloodlust, the need for battle hums in my veins.

But when I'm with Sadie, all that pressure lightens. I forget that I'm a killer. I can remember that my wolf isn't just a weapon, he's a wild creature, and there's more to life than fighting.

CHAPTER 6

adie

CAREER DAY COMES, and my students haven't been this excited since I brought them the jackalope toy. I have them sit in a circle and caution them to be on their best behavior, but when the four towering soldiers arrive, the classroom erupts with excitement. I try to smooth my features but can't stop smiling either, as my heart thumps wildly. As usual, Rafe takes the lead, greeting me and addressing the class in a smooth, deep voice that settles the children faster than I ever could. Deke hovers in the back. He's stone-faced and silent. Not once does he look my way, which is fine. I need to focus.

Rafe introduces his brother, Lance, and I recognize the blond from the alleyway. He winks at me, and I narrow my eyes at him. The fourth and final member of the group is Channing, who waves to the class before crossing his arms in front of his chest, making his biceps pop even bigger. All four of our guests look badass in a mix of camo and civilian clothes. Deke's in an unbuttoned camo shirt with the long sleeves rolled up. Underneath he's in his usual outfit of black jeans and t-shirt.

I tear my eyes away from him and get back to doing my job. "Everyone, this is Mr. Rafe Lightfoot. He and his friends are here to talk to us today about their service in the Army. But first, can we name the four branches of the military?"

The kids sing-song "Army, Navy, Airforce, Marines," in dutiful chorus. Except for Jackson in the back, who thinks it's funny to replace "Marines with "GI Joes." The two kids next to him immediately inform him, "That's wrong. It's the Marines," and I have to settle their squabble before things get too heated.

"The Army's the best," little Owen in the front row pipes up. "My dad said so."

Rafe crouches right down in front of Owen, his eyes crinkling. "Can I tell you a secret?"

Owen nods, wide eyed.

"Your dad is right. But it's a secret. Don't tell anyone. Because then the service members in the Airforce, Navy and Marines will be jealous, and they'll all want to become soldiers like us." He winks at Owen, who's overcome with awe and rises. "Every branch of the military is important. We all make a team. Teamwork is important."

For the rest of Rafe's talk, I fight to keep from looking over at Deke. I lose the battle, but when I glance over, he's wearing his shades over his eyes. Lance notices my attention and gives me another wink. I roll my eyes.

Rafe is almost done, and the class is getting restless, ready for recess.

"Do you have any questions for Mr. Rafe and his friends?" I ask. Ten hands shoot up. Owen has both his hands up when I call on him.

"Did you shoot lotsa bad guys?" he asks, and there's a swell of sound from the rest of the class, who are excited by the prospect of learning about violence.

"Sometimes," Rafe answers seriously. "But only if we were sure they were bad guys, and we had done everything else we could to keep the peace."

"Do you have lotsa guns?" Owen asks at the same time Jackson shouts from the back. "Did they die right away? Was there lots of blood?"

"Okay, that's enough questions!" I trill. "It's time for recess. Everyone say, *thank you, Mr. Rafe*."

"Thank you, Mr. Rafe," half the class singsongs. The rest want to know the answers to Jackon's questions. I had no idea they were so bloodthirsty. My teacher aide comes to help the kids into their coats for recess. I'm caught up in a swirling eddy of brightly-clothed children, but head over to Rafe as soon as I escape the tide.

"Thanks again," I say.

"No problem. Great kids."

"You guys are great with them." Out of the corner of my eye, I see Owen approaching Deke. The big soldier kneels to help the kindergartener tie his shoes, and my ovaries melt.

And as I leave for the day, I'm even more determined to figure out what's going on with Deke. What's stopping him from getting close? It's like he has this big secret, something he's keeping from me and the rest of the world. And I just want to throw my arms around him and tell him I don't care.

That's what I'll do, I decide as I get in my car to drive home that night. I'll lure him out and seduce him. Or something. Enough of this sitting around. I'm all in on Operation Deke.

I just have to figure out how to do it.

Normally, I'd call up my girlfriends and get them to

come over for wine and a brainstorming session, but they're super busy right now. Adele is taking more catering jobs to cover the slow season at the chocolate shop, and Tabitha is helping her. Charlie is busy too, with some secret project she's not telling any of us about. Besides, they're not entirely pro-Deke. They're firmly pro-Sadie and seem to think I don't know what I'm doing when it comes to him. I get it—I haven't made the best choices when it comes to men. They don't want me to get bulldozed by a domineering man again.

Deke isn't like that. He's strong, but he doesn't bulldoze me. Besides, he's not even interested or available for a relationship. He can be my wild fling.

I've never had a wild fling.

I've never been wild. And Deke definitely makes me feel wild. In the most wonderful way.

I get home, kick off my ballet flats and rub my hands together. I'm about to call Deke when I see I've missed a call, and I've got a voicemail.

My heart sinks. It's from my father. "Sadie, we need to talk."

THIRTY MINUTES LATER, I pull into the parking lot of the uptight restaurant my father likes. I didn't have time to dress up as I know my father would like, but I changed into a fancier cardigan and ballet flats. My battle dress. Too bad I can't roll up in a tank and wear a suit of armor. Not that my father can't pierce those sorts of shields. I square my shoulders and march inside.

My father's already seated at a table right in the center of the restaurant, where everyone can see him. He's town councilman and prides himself on knowing everyone "worth knowing," as he'd put it.

He introduced me to Scott.

"Darling," he says as I dutifully cross to him and bend down to give his cheek a kiss. "I took the liberty of ordering already." He gestures for me to sit.

"Great." I'll have to pick at whatever he ordered for me. Last time it was freshwater trout and a salad of mostly arugula. I hate fish and a little arugula goes a long way.

I look longingly at my wine glass but shake my head when the waiter offers a drink menu. I'm a total lightweight. Besides, I only drink in public with people I absolutely trust not to mock me, like my girl posse. When I was out with Scott, I ordered a lot of cranberry juice with club soda. With my father, I don't bother with a mocktail. He'll drink enough for the both of us.

My father is commonly a handsome man, with silver tinsel in his hair. He's tan and fit from golf at the country club and skiing in the winter. He's already getting a few appreciative looks from two forty or fifty-something ladies with yoga tight bodies and Botox tight faces. They keep glancing over at him, and he pretends not to notice, but I know he does. He perfected the art of hiding his wandering eye back when he was married to my mother. Now it's a habit of his to pretend to be oblivious to other women's attention, at least in public.

Another similarity he shares with Scott.

I clear my throat. "You said you wanted to speak to me?"

"I did." We're both absorbed in separate tasks, me placing my napkin on my lap and him inspecting his whiskey glass. We've yet to really make eye contact. All part of our regular farce of a father-daughter dinner. "How was work?"

"Wonderful." He doesn't care about my teaching career, so I skip telling the latest stories about the moments this week when my students were particularly cute. He doesn't deserve them. "How's yours?"

He launches into some city council story, and I nod and murmur at the correct places like a dutiful daughter. Another thing Scott had in common with my father. All their stories revolved around work or golf but mainly them being Very Important. That and their stories seem to get longer and more boring each time.

About twenty minutes into the story, my father clears his throat. "That's the project Scott proposed, by the way," he says, seemingly casually, but he makes eye contact with me for the first time. "Have you seen him?"

"Who?" I am busy making a big show of cutting into my trout. Poor dead fish, sacrificed to this dreadful dinner. I wish I could go back in time and toss it back into its mountain stream. Then one of us would be free.

My father clears his throat again. "Scott Sears. Your boyfriend."

"Ex-boyfriend," I say with a big smile. Probably should tone it down, but I am very happy Scott is my ex.

"Really? That's a shame." My father signals for another single malt scotch. "I thought things were going well."

"Mmm." I pretend my mouth is full of arugula.

"Actually, that's why I called you here. I wanted to talk to you about Scott." He gives me a look under his thick brows, a look that means *I am very serious. We are having a Very Important Talk.* "He's a good man, Sadie. There aren't that many in a town this small. He's going places. He's an important part of the growth and development of the town. I think you'd be very happy with him."

Seriously?

"When you decided to become a teacher, as you know, your mother and I were concerned."

I grip my fork tighter to keep me from going for my knife. I hate it when my father talks about mom like he knows her and can speak for her opinion. As far as I know, he and mom haven't spoken in years.

"But we thought if you could find yourself a good man with a stable vocation, you'd be fine. Besides, once you start having children, you'll want a man to support you."

I can't even.

"And, Sadie, Scott is that man." My father starts rambling again, and I resist the urge to roll my eyes. Which is so unlike me, but what am I doing here? It would be so easy to just stand up, throw my napkin down on my mangled entree and stride away from the table. I could even grab a bottle of wine on the way out. I don't need to drive home—I could call Deke. Tell him I need a ride, and that I'll owe him another favor. He'll ride up on his big bike just as I'm finishing the wine, hand me a helmet, and I'll straddle that giant, vibrating beast, all that power between my legs and...*Mmmmm.*

I'm halfway through a motorcycle-ride-with-Deke fantasy when my father says. "And of course, there's the wedding. You'll need to iron things out before you two travel together."

I've half tuned my father out, but this snags my attention. "Wedding?" Oh God! How could I forget Jenn's wedding? I blocked it out.

My father steeples his fingers and purses his lips to signal his displeasure. He can tell I haven't been paying attention. "Aren't you two both in a wedding together? For your two friends in Santa Fe?"

Gaaaaaaah. "Jenn and Geoff. Yes." I resist the urge to rub my head. Suddenly I've got a headache. Jenn is a high school friend from Taos. Her boyfriend Geoff is Scott's friend from college. They're the ones who set us up with each other when Scott first moved to Taos from Santa Fe.

"You'll be in Santa Fe for a long weekend, right?"

I suddenly realize why my father looks so smug, why he knows all about this wedding and organized this dinner with me.

"You talked to Scott," I accuse. "He called you and told you all about this. That's why you wanted to talk to me."

My father frowns again. "Scott and I talked, yes. He's involved in business around Taos, as am I. And our paths cross often."

"Of course. You're birds of a feather."

I don't mean it as a compliment, but my father takes it as one. "Yes. And he mentioned this wedding, that you'll be spending time together in an idyllic setting. It'll be the perfect time to talk about your relationship and smooth out your differences."

Only my father would refer to Scott cheating on me and being a total butthole as "differences" and expect us to simply "smooth them out," meaning he expects me to overlook them. Like my mother overlooked my father's indiscretions until she finally got the courage to leave him.

"It's perfect," my father continues. He's all jovial now, cutting his steak. "I always said you and Scott were meant to be."

I would do my best impression of Munch's painting *The Scream*, vocals and all, but I am truly speechless.

"I'm your father," he finishes. "I simply want what's best for you."

WHEN I FINALLY STAGGER BACK HOME, I have a splitting headache. Dinners with my father are always like descending to the Ninth Circle of hell, but that was something else.

Apparently my father's vision for me is to become some sort of 1950s desperate housewife. And Scott would heartily approve.

They colluded on this. I found my backbone to stand up to Scott, but the two of them working in tandem? It's just too much. I don't know—I've always been a doormat to my dad. He has a very dominant personality. After he drove my mom away, and he was all I had, I think I was afraid of ever displeasing him for fear the only parent I had would reject me.

It's old, stupid stuff, but the resonance is still present in every conversation and interaction we have. He's telling me what to do with my life, and I'm doing my best not to get steamrolled.

But I have more pressing problems than learning to stand up to him. The wedding is two weekends away. Scott and I and the rest of the wedding party are all expected to be at a resort in Santa Fe for a long weekend. I know Jenn's family spared no expense. The groom's family comes from money too, which is why Scott was so excited to be involved.

I'm going to have to put on a bridesmaid's dress and big smile and stand across from Scott. He'll have three days and two nights to harangue me about dating him again. He's probably the groomsman escorting me down the aisle. Jenn planned this all when she thought we'd be together. She even joked about it being a trial run for Scott and I. I never told her about the cheating.

Why did I let the farce between me and Scott run so long? Because I was too nice to end things, even though I wasn't interested. I hate hurting people's feelings. And now that I think about it, some of the feelings I was worried about hurting belonged to Jenn and Geoff. Like I owed them to keep dating their friend just because they set us up.

God, I really am a pleaser!

Obviously Scott doesn't share that trait. Control and criticism are his favorite relationship tools. And cheating. The only thing I got out of the relationship was my father's approval.

This is an all-out emergency. I'm tempted to call Jenn and claim I have mono. But she doesn't deserve that. And I've already taken time off for the wedding.

There's just one thing to do. I gulp down a glass of wine, and pull up Deke and my text chat on my phone.

Here goes nothing.

"I need another favor," I text him. "But it's big. Really big."

Ten seconds later, my cell phone rings.

"What do you need?" Deke asks. No *hello*, no preamble, no nothing. I take a deep breath. I should've drunk more wine.

"Sadie, you okay?"

"Yeah, yeah, I'm fine."

"Is it Sears?"

"Scott? No. Well, not exactly. But I have to ask you for a favor. A huge one."

There's a pause where I remember what he asked in return for the last favor. As if he's thinking the same thing, his voice softens. "Yeah, baby?"

Crap, now I'm super turned on. "Um, yeah."

"How big?"

"Really big. I would owe you so much. On top of what I already do."

"I'm sure we can work something out." He sounds playful. OMG, we're flirting now! I flop down on my bed.

"Maybe."

"What is it? Just tell me."

"I need a date to a wedding," I say and continue in a rush before I lose my nerve. "A pretend date again—not a real one," I add quickly.

"Pretend." Does he sound disappointed?

"Um, it's at a resort in Santa Fe, so it would be for the whole weekend. I'm in the wedding party, so I have to go a day early. Scott will be there. He and I were going to go together, but—"

"Say no more," Deke says.

"Really?" I feel as if a fifty pound dumbbell lifted off my chest. "You'll do it?"

"Babe," is all he says to that. I take it to mean: *Of course.* "When is it?"

"Two weeks from Thursday. I already got the time off, but I pushed it out of my mind because I didn't want to deal with it." I give him the details. "I can drive, but I don't think you'll be comfortable in my little car."

"I'll drive. What time should I pick you up Thursday?"

"Um, are you sure?"

"Yep. What time?"

"Around noon?"

"I'll be there."

"Thank you so much. I owe you big time."

"Mmm." His voice is a dark rumbling hum. Like he loves the idea of me owing him. Or like he's going to collect more than a kiss this time.

Oh God, I really hope so! I liked the last favor he cashed in with me.

"Do you have a suit to wear?"

"Babe," he says again and hangs up.

I laugh into the disconnected phone. Deke is like no man I have ever met.

~

Deke

My dick is hard by the time I hang up with Sadie, my thoughts of collecting on favors turning dirty fast.

Oh shit. What did I just get myself into? I disobeyed a direct order from my alpha by agreeing to go with Sadie.

But there was no fucking way I was going to let her down. No fucking way I'd let her spend a long weekend with her ex as her date when she doesn't want to.

My wolf already wants to tear that guy apart for bothering her.

Spending an entire weekend in close quarters with humans—at a wedding, no less—is a special kind of hell for me, but for Sadie, I'd do anything. I'll keep my wolf in check. I'll try to act civilized. Speak in full sentences. Make a decent impression as her fake boyfriend. Hell, I'll even find a goddamn suit.

I stand, a shiver of pleasure running through me, coming straight from my wolf. I sense his desire to yip and spin around.

Well, I'll be damned.

My wolf is happy. Excited, even.

I walk out of the lodge and down to the river, hiking uphill along the bank to release some of the pent-up energy. I need to figure out what I'm going to tell Rafe. How to present this.

It's a mission. Not a date.

I'm not engaging with a human on a social basis. It's a job.

A half mile up, I come across Lance fishing in the stream.

I shake my head because I seriously don't get it. We're predators. We hunt animals on four legs. We don't need to stand at the water's edge in human form with a fishing pole to catch food.

"Don't say it," Lance murmurs, correctly reading my thoughts. I presume he's speaking quietly to not scare off the fish.

"I didn't say a word." I stand beside him. The sounds of the wilderness register as peaceful for once. I always crave the wild, and I absolutely love living here where we can roam the mountain on four paws or two wheels at any moment, but this afternoon feels different.

Like I almost understand Lance's urge to fish. It's not about the catch. It's about the quiet. Standing at the cold water's edge and watching it babble by. Listening to the trees.

Why is my wolf so calm?

Sadie, I almost hear him whisper.

I shake my head. I can't have Sadie. Sadie's not for keeping.

Lance shoots me a curious look. "You seem… different."

I don't answer. I can't tell him about Sadie because there's nothing going on. And nothing will go on.

"It's the teacher, isn't it?"

I draw in a sharp breath at the mere mention of her.

"She calms the madness," I finally admit.

"She seems sweet."

Just hearing him talk about her makes my heart surge up and bounce in my chest. "She is," I say gruffly. "But it's not like that. I'm not getting involved."

"Right." Lance looks into the river, probably so I don't have to lie to his face.

"Her ex is bothering her," I explain. "And she asked me to pretend to be her boyfriend to scare him off."

Now Lance looks over and his brows pop up in surprise. "Yeah?"

"Yeah." I scrub a hand over my face.

"Fuck, Deke. That sounds like trouble. Does she know you're likely to put that ex of hers in a body bag?"

A sick feeling stirs in my gut. "That won't happen," I say gruffly although I'm not even half sure that's true.

If that guy laid one fucking hand on her, I would kill him. No question.

But that doesn't seem to be the nature of her perturbance. The fact that she doesn't seem too hurt by the guy in general soothes my wolf's need to exact justice for her. It seems like he's more of an annoyance than a real threat—to her heart or to her person.

"I don't know, Deke. The last human female you protected landed you with an assault and battery charge. And you would've flat-out killed the guy if we hadn't been there. I'm not saying you weren't justified, I just—"

"I know," I snap. "I lose control. My wolf goes into war-mode in every situation."

"I would hate for that sweet teacher to ever see that side of you," Lance says in a gentle voice. "That's all."

A low growl rumbles from my chest. I actually think my wolf is growling at the idea of me scaring Sadie. It's true I would want to punch my own face if that ever happened.

"I won't touch the ex," I vow. "But I'm not going to refuse Sadie the favor."

I couldn't.

I feel bad I'm leaving for the weekend when the team is trying to discover how we got made in Switzerland, but at the moment it feels like we're chasing shadows, and Sadie needs me.

"I get it." Lance snags a fish on his hook and tugs, pulling a flopping rainbow trout out of the water.

I rumble my appreciation. If he catches a few more, we can all have fish for dinner. He gently withdraws the hook and drops the fish in his net in the water. "Just be careful. I like Sadie—"

He breaks off when a ferocious growl erupts from my throat.

"Not in that way," he says quickly. "Not at all. Dude— that's what I"m talking about. I don't know if you can pull this off."

Shit. He may be right. But backing out now is not an option.

"I'll pull it off," I swear. "Sadie will be safe with me."

CHAPTER 7

adie

My belly is full of butterflies on the day of the wedding trip. I only told my friends about my plus-one to the wedding but not my dad or even Scott, who tried very hard to get me to drive with him. I knew if I told Scott, he'd go running to my dad, and I didn't want to deal with the mountain of judgement that would crash down on my head over associating myself so closely with what my dad would clearly describe as an unsavory character.

The day dawns bright and beautiful. I take a long shower and shave my legs. I can take my time because I'm not rushing off to school. I left the substitute for my class with full lesson plans, so everything should be fine in there. So long as she or he has experience with younger students.

I consider things, and then I shave a little extra. I packed my good underwear. I tell myself the extra silky thongs are so

I don't show panty lines under the bridesmaid dress. *Sure they are.* My ovaries aren't fooled.

For the drive, I'm in a sweater and yoga pants and my cute grey faux fur lined boots that double as hiking boots. The resort has private trails, and I'm sure Deke and I will have time to slip away and hike one of them. I get the feeling he likes nature. I remember how nice it was when he took me to the bridge on his bike.

If we have some time alone, will he cash in on the favor again? Ask for a kiss… or something more?

I'm sure we can work something out.

Maybe I should ask him. Just tell him what I want. I'll make it clear I have no expectations. That I know it's not a real date. That he'd be doing me another favor. The resort has a spa and outdoor hot tub. I packed a bikini just in case.

And I won't let Scott spoil our fun. I'm hoping he'll see Deke with me and leave me alone the rest of the weekend.

"Don't you want to play?" crackles a creepy voice in the corner. I jump and whirl at the same time, but it's only the stupid Jackalope toy in the corner. It's been malfunctioning, going off at odd moments unprompted, so I brought it home from my classroom. Probably shouldn't have bought it from a sketchy knockoff toy warehouse online.

A roar of an engine outside gives me a shiver. *Deke.* I toss the Jackalope into my bedroom closet and grab my suitcase.

Deke's car is a big, black, boxy-style Mercedes with a suped up engine. Loud and growly, like his bike. He's already out of the driver's seat and coming around to meet me. He's wearing his usual biker man outfit—big boots and faded T, black jeans and bad ass smirk. Of course, he's not dressing up for the weekend.

Oh my God—I was nuts to ask him to be my date. The entire wedding party will think I've lost my mind.

Have I? I may have. My sexy little pink thong's already wet. I fumble with my keys but by some miracle lock the door and race down to meet him.

"Deke." I'm so short compared to him, I have to dance up on my toes to greet him. I throw my arms around his neck because I'm absurdly glad to see him. Because I want to thank him for doing this favor for me.

He stiffens for just a moment, and I realize I've overstepped. It's not a real date, of course. I shouldn't act so friendly. But then he wraps a big hand around the back of my neck, tugs me to tiptoe and kisses me right there in front of my townhouse. In broad daylight, in front of my neighbors—and after a second with my lips pressed to his firm ones, I don't care. His mouth is warm on mine, dominating but not demanding. His breath is a little minty.

He tilts me backwards, so I'm just the tiniest bit off balance. Without thinking, I drop my suitcase and grab on to his giant biceps to hang on. His cock bulges in his pants, twitching against my belly.

I'd happily call the whole weekend off just so we can stand here and smooch. He breaks the kiss but doesn't back away. Instead he presses his forehead to mine for a moment.

"Sadie," his deep voice rumbles through me. His eyes are bright green in the sunlight. My ovaries swoon.

He backs up and helps me straighten, picking my suitcase up and supporting me with his free hand at my back.

Oh my.

"Good idea," I say breathlessly once I'm in the car and Deke's returned from putting my suitcase in the back. He also held the door for me and buckled me in, which is good because my limbs are jelly after that kiss. My heart is still fluttering. My ovaries are still out cold. "We should practice being boyfriend and girlfriend, just in case people ask."

"Practice… yeah, definitely." He puts his G-wagon in gear, and we're off. In a few minutes, we're flying down the road to the highway.

"I think it's a good idea," I insist, trying to calm the flapping butterfly wings in my belly from the kiss. "People are going to think I'm still with Scott. We'll have to explain."

"Will there be a quiz?"

"Maybe." I frown at that. "They all know Scott. They're his type of people."

Deke grunts at that, and I feel even more unhappy. Jenn is a good friend, but what if the rest take Scott's side? They've got that upper class way of being rude and condescending in the politest way possible. Under their polo shirts and shiny smiles is coiled razor wire.

"Sadie," Deke calls, and I realize I've been staring out the window. The glass reflects the worry lines in my forehead. "Relax," he settles his hand on my knee and squeezes.

And I do, settling into the plush seat. For a rugged military-looking vehicle, the interiors are pretty posh.

"And we can definitely practice, if you want." His voice sounds lower and rougher than usual. Another squeeze of my knee, and arousal spreads through me.

"Practice does make perfect," I trill. Who cares if Scott's friends don't approve of my life choices? Deke will protect me. Some rebellious part of me I never knew existed sort of revels in the idea of shocking everyone at that wedding this weekend.

And who knows, when we're in private, I might even shock myself with my behavior.

I shiver and do a surreptitious butt wriggle.

"Cold?" Deke turns on the fancy seat warmers. He ups the cab temperature and makes sure the warm air is blowing my way.

"This is good, thanks," I say.

"Sure? I got a blanket in the back." He reaches behind my seat, rummages around then hands me a water bottle. "I also brought snacks."

"You did?" He's so freaking thoughtful. "This is perfect, thank you. I take it back. You don't need to practice." I smile at him. "You're already the perfect fake boyfriend. Way better than Scott."

Deke snorts. "That's probably not hard. I can't imagine that guy paying attention to anyone besides himself." He signals his turn before getting on the highway out of town. "None of my business, babe, but what did you see in him?"

"I've been asking myself the same question. I think I only dated him because my father wanted it. And I think he only dated me to align with my father."

"No love lost, then?"

"No. I think I tried to believe I loved him, but… yeah. I don't think it was love. I just didn't want to make waves with a break-up. So when he cheated on me, it was a relief."

"He *cheated on you*?" Deke says incredulously, like I'm some kind of sex goddess no man would ever stray from.

"Yep. But like I said, I was glad. Good reason to do what I secretly knew I should've done two years earlier."

"You close with your dad?"

"Not at all. The opposite, but when my mom left, he sued for full custody. She let him have it, even though I wanted to go with her."

"That sucks," he says softly after I've fallen silent.

"It was a long time ago. Okay, let's get our stories straight," I say as Deke guns it past the mountain. "How did we meet? What do we say?"

"The truth. I saw you across the plaza, and I wanted you."

I flush. "You wanted to *meet* me."

He suppresses a grin and says, "Sure."

A fire kindles between my legs. I squeeze my inner thighs together and clear my throat. "And I saw you with your biker friends and wanted to meet you too. And for our first date you took me on a bike ride. Then home, but you were a perfect gentleman."

"Babe," he looks pained. "Don't tell them that."

"You are the perfect gentleman. And you ride a motorcycle and drive the type of car all the rap songs sing about."

This gets a real grin. "You listen to rap?"

"Not a lot. I used to think *Shawty* was a rapper that all the other rappers knew. That's how much I know about rap."

It's a long time before Deke stops chuckling at that one. I might have encouraged it by singing the first few lines of *In Da Club* by 50 cent, and explaining that I thought the song was about his friend Shawty celebrating a birthday.

"So that's settled," I say a few hours later, as we turn into the resort entrance. "That's our story. We just stick to it, and it'll be fine." But when we pull up to the lodge, I feel my face stiffening into a frozen smile. There are tons of fancy cars being valeted—Porsches, Land Rovers, even a Maserati. Big money, fast cars, people in expensive clothes drinking too much and pretending they're important—this is my dad's world. He'd be rubbing his hands together at all the potential business contacts. He'd see this wedding as a networking event.

Scott definitely will be working the crowd while he's here. I can almost hear him lecturing me on how to behave, so he can make a good impression. My shoulders rise towards my ears, stiffening in defense at the memory.

Scott wanted a Stepford Wife and made it clear I couldn't quite fit the part. I was always a little off, too honest, too quirky, too much of myself. He and my dad always tried to iron out the lumps in my personality. They squashed me down, but I could never lie flat.

Like a doormat.

I yank open the door and jump out of the wagon before Deke can come around and let me out.

"Relax," he takes my hand, his big one enveloping mine. "It's gonna be okay."

"Of course," I say, but my calm is as fake as our relationship.

Deke

I'M NOT sure the last time I felt so light. Sadie makes me laugh. She's fucking *adorable.*

The resort is set in the foothills of the Sangre de Cristos. I might be able to slip away and go for a run, maybe. Work some of this pent-up lust out of my system. I'd love to run now, but Sadie's too keyed up, and it's making all my protective instincts surge out of control. Which is a recipe for disaster.

Lance was right. If Sears even comes near her, I could lose it.

And that kill wouldn't be one I'd survive. Rafe would have to put me down for good.

I put a protective arm around her as we cross the lobby. She leans into me almost unconsciously. *Win.* By the time we get to the front desk, she's smiling again, a genuine smile, not that pinched awful thing that clashed with the anxiety in her scent.

My presence seems to help her tension. Maybe I can try

other ways to relax her. If she'll let me. I need to think of this as a job. I'm here with a mission—be Sadie's fake date. Protect her from her ex. I'm not here to mate her, despite what my wolf seems to think.

"We'll need to add an extra room," she tells the front desk person. "I called about it earlier."

"I'm sorry miss, we're at 100 percent occupancy." The front desk guy eyes me, and I tighten my hold on Sadie's shoulder.

Sadie shoots me a glance. "But when I called that's not what you said."

I keep quiet as Sadie and the resort receptionist try to figure it out. My wolf is fist-pumping the whole time. He doesn't mind sharing a room, a bed. Hell, he was looking forward to it. But he's not the one who has to hold back. To try not to claim Sadie the second I get her alone. Sink my teeth in that sweet-scented flesh of hers and permanently mark her as mine.

"Deke, I'm sorry." Sadie turns to me, chewing her lip. "There's only one room."

"Babe. It'll be fine." I say and run my thumb over that worried lower lip. Her pupils dilate and arousal flares in her scent. "We'll work it out," I promise.

I'll give you a workout. My dick is stiff in my jeans.

"Besides, isn't this good? People won't wonder about the status of our relationship. They'll believe… we're together." I swallow what I was about to say. *They'll know you're mine.* My wolf wants to howl the news until the lodge rafters shake. I'm going to have to work hard to keep him in check. Especially if we're sleeping in the same room together.

"You're right. This is good. It's fine. It's all fine."

I make a light circle on her lower back with my palm as she convinces herself. I hate seeing her agitated. She sighs and turns into me, and my arms shoot around her like I was made to hug her. I grit my teeth and hope my dick doesn't skewer her belly. But when Sadie melts against me it's all worth it.

"Feel better?" I murmur into her hair.

"Yes. Thank you." She smiles up at me, and fuck if I don't want to kiss her here, now, in front of everyone. Trouble is, I wouldn't stop with a kiss.

"Sadie," I murmur, and then my muscles stiffen as I get whiff of Douchebag Cologne. Or whatever gag-awful scent Sadie's ex is wearing. I look over Sadie's head and sure enough, there's Scott Sears swaggering in his preppy clothes.

Part of me wants to throw Sadie over my shoulder and race up the stairs to our room. The other part of me wants to throw Scott out of the lodge. He's wearing hiking boots that look expensive but never worn. Not a speck of mud on them. How long would this douchebag actually survive on a wilderness trek? My wolf wants to chase him down the mountain and find out.

"Incoming," I whisper into Sadie's ear. "Hold tight to me."

Sadie's brows knit together in confusion, but she clings tighter, with her arm around my middle. I tuck her right to my side, under my arm, and damn if she doesn't fit perfectly. Then she sees who I'm talking about.

"Oh," she breathes.

"You got this." I nuzzle her head.

"Sadie?" Scott spots us by the front desk. His gaze bounces from me to her. Emotions flit over his face in comical progression—surprise, annoyance, anger—and settle on fake happy. "It's so good to see you here." He sounds smooth and casual, but he doesn't look at me, and his scent stays angry.

"Yeah, I took the day off work. Deke drove us down." She turns further into my body and puts her hand on my chest, giving me a little smile that I can't help but return. "We had such a great road trip. He made it perfect."

Scott looks like he got a whiff of roadkill. His fake smile slips a little bit.

"Thanks, babe." I squeeze her close and dip my head to breathe in her sweet scent. She's totally sincere. She looks back at Scott, though, and her scent changes. I think she feels a little bad for Scott.

"I hope this won't be too awkward for us," Sadie says.

"No, no," Scott forces out. "I'm actually seeing someone now. She's a model. She's going to try to get away to meet me here."

"Oh, that's wonderful," Sadie says. Not a whiff of jealousy in her scent. Just relief.

Scott, however, is lying. He pulls out his phone and waves it. "I, uh, gotta take this," he says, even though his phone is not ringing. "See you tonight?"

"Yes." Sadie waves, and I steer her towards the grand staircase. The bellhop already took our bags to our room.

As we ascend, I look back down at Scott. He's ducked in the corner, hunched and on the phone, probably phoning an escort service to see if he can drum up a weekend date. Heh.

Score one for the fucked up werewolf.

CHAPTER 8

eke

OUR ROOM IS bright and spacious, with a view of the mountains, which sprawl just outside. I'm relieved. I might be able to hike far enough out to shift and run to take the edge off. Tight quarters and too many humans make me antsy. Not to mention the sexual tension.

Even as I think about leaving for a run, though, my wolf resists.

Like he's not willing to leave Sadie's side, even for a minute. The urge to protect her is overwhelming.

I stand at the window while Sadie moves around, unpacking. For such a small person, Sadie takes up ten times as much space as you'd expect her to. It's her scent, her sunny energy and her smile. The rest is clothes. She brought a lot of clothes for a four day trip.

"That went well." She bustles back and forth between the bathroom and the bedroom, spreading her stuff everywhere.

Good thing the room is big. There's a nice king bed made of rustic logs that should be sturdy enough to take what I'm capable of dishing out.

I shake my head to dismiss that thought. We're in the same room, but I'm going to be a gentleman. I'll sleep on the floor.

Unless she makes the first move, my wolf counters.

"I think we should be fine this weekend. Scott should leave me alone with you here."

"He better," I grunt. I hate hearing his name on her lips. He doesn't deserve her time and attention. *Neither do I,* I remind myself.

Sadie wrinkles her nose. "Do you think he really has a new girlfriend?"

"Nope." I turn from the window and uncross my arms, so I look less intimidating.

Sadie's lips quirk, and her eyes dance with amusement. "You think he was lying?"

She's so trusting, it's cute. Except that dickbags like Scott take advantage of her. I give her a soft look. "Babe."

"Oh. I guess it couldn't be that easy." She gnaws her lip again.

A knock sounds on the door. "Room service," a helpful voice trills outside.

Even though it's probably not a danger, I stride to the door before Sadie can get there, my need to play bodyguard raging.

"Sadie Diaz?" The lady's brows shoot up when her gaze meets my chest and then has to rise to find my face.

"Yes," Sadie calls from behind me.

The woman uncovers a tray of fresh chocolate strawberries. There's a note with them. "From your secret admirer," she gushes, winking at me like I sent them.

Dammit. The thought hadn't occurred to me. I'm not sure I even knew that was a thing until this moment. But Sadie sure as hell deserves them, even if they are from her dickwad ex.

"Oh," Sadie says without much enthusiasm. She shoots me an apologetic look. "Great."

I take the tray and shut the door.

Sadie opens the card. "*Enjoy your stay. Let's talk soon*," she reads the note aloud.

I try to keep from growling out loud.

"Yuck. This is so like Scott. He doesn't stalk in ordinary ways. He throws his money around and puts apps on my phone and then just won't leave me alone even though I have you here. I'm obviously with you, but he has to prove he's the bigger man with a bigger bank account or something—"

"Huh. He's pretty brave. Does he think I won't rip his arms off for moving in on my fake girlfriend?"

Sadie lets out a soft laugh, the awkward tension leaving her.

"Hey." I cross and settle my hands on either side of her head, cupping her cheeks. "I'll keep him away from you."

"Thanks. I'm so glad you came with me. I was absolutely dreading this weekend, but now..."

"Now what?" I don't know why her answer seems important. Mission critical, even.

She flushes and shrugs. "It seems like it might be fun."

My dick punches out against my zipper. Fun is definitely on the agenda for me, too.

For Sadie, of course. I'm not here for me. It's all part of the mission.

And if that mission involves giving Sadie Diaz orgasms until she screams, so be it.

Sadie

There's a second sharp rap on the door. I open it and greet the bellhop, who's delivering a welcome basket from the bride and groom. "Welcome reception at five," he reminds me, and I thank him.

"Welcome basket delivery." I set it down and unpack it. "Oh good, there's a folder with our itinerary for the weekend." I set that aside. The rest of the basket is all fun stuff, and I announce each item like a dork. "We also got champagne and hand engraved glasses." The glasses read *Whine on*." Jenn has come to our Whine Wednesdays when she's in Taos. "And this cute little white bag that reads *bridesmaid*, slippers—I can use those for the spa day." I'm babbling now, but Deke's listening.

I heave a giant sigh. "I'm just trying to figure out how it's going to go."

"It?" Deke stands right behind me, making goosebumps race across my skin.

"This weekend. This whole thing. I need structure, Deke. I need a plan."

He cocks his head to the side, his dark eyes squinting at me for a moment. Then he says, "Okay."

"Okay?"

He waves a big hand. "Talk me through it."

"Really? You're not going to just tell me to go with the flow?" He seems like that sort of guy.

"This is our mission. We never go into a mission without a plan. Of course, when things go sideways, we have to improvise."

I grab the folder and flip it open. "Our theme is "Romantic rustic," I read aloud. "The attire is "Mountain Chic" I turn to Deke and ask with fake seriousness, "Are all your outfits Mountain Chic?"

"Don't know what that means, but I doubt it." His lips quirk.

I grin back, feeling better already. Deke makes it all better.

"Well, all my outfits are mountain chic, so we'll be fine." I turn back to the itinerary to read through it. The bed creaks as Deke shifts positions. His weight makes the bed dip, and I half roll into him. Now we're face to face, close enough to kiss.

"Is that what you call this?" he murmurs. His fingers pluck at my little yoga top.

I feel his touch through my clothes. My core clenches. "No, this is athleisure wear."

"Don't know what that is, either."

"Fancy workout clothes. I've also got a closet full of off-duty kindergarten teacher chic. Mostly jeans, ballet flats and cardigans." I shift a little closer to him. A few more inches, and my breasts will touch his chest. Not that I'm intensely aware of that fact or anything. "I'm sure you're super interested in all my fashion choices."

"Maybe I am." His hot breath warms my face. His finger traces the neckline of my shirt. "But I admit, I'm more interested in what's underneath."

My nipples tighten. "Oh yeah?" I'd move even closer, but then I'd be actually climbing him. *DO IT!* My ovaries shout. They hold up a sign that reads: *GET THE DICK.*

"I have to confess, this is not my usual op, but I am definitely up to the unique challenges it presents." His eyes crinkle.

I laugh. "I know one of those challenges is putting up with my anxiety." I grab the itinerary and toss it away.

"Oh, I think I know what to do with your anxiety," he murmurs.

I shoot him an inquisitive look, but he's rubbing his face, looking away like he didn't mean to let that slip out.

The rest of the basket is filled with snacks and spa samples. There's also a note from Jenn thanking me for being a part of her and Geoff's special day. Plus a personalized calendar with pictures of Jenn and me and Geoff. Unfortunately Scott is in a lot of them. Ugh.

"I've never been to a wedding," Deke rumbles. "Is this typical?"

"Unfortunately, yes. The average wedding cost is like thirty thousand." Jenn and Geoff are definitely spending way more.

"Jesus. You gonna do this?" He waves a hand at the basket.

"Um, do what? Use the spa samples?"

"Get married. Spend thirty thousand on a wedding."

"Ummmmm." My brain shorts out. "I want to get married. One day. I want kids. And my dad will probably insist on a big fancy wedding for networking purposes."

"Fuck your dad," Deke says with such beautiful nonchalance I want to record him, so I can play it over and over again with a beat track. "Don't care about him. What do you want?"

Suddenly, I get this image of me and Deke standing on a mountain top, holding hands. I'm in a cute but simple white summer dress, and Deke's in his usual attire. My girlfriends and Deke's biker buddies stand behind us, clapping. Rafe's the officiant, and after Deke and I kiss, we all head to picnic tables for barbecue. Simple. Casual. Beautiful. I feel it with such a strong sense of longing. And suddenly there are tears in my eyes because it's all I want.

Eek—too clingy. Deke said he doesn't do relationships. He's going to be a fling for me. Just a fling.

"I'd prefer something more casual," I whisper. "Outside. A few friends, maybe my mom. An officiant and a picnic afterwards. That's it." I summon my courage and ask, "What about you? What's your dream wedding?"

"Never getting married," he says, and my dreams die with a little sad trombone sound. "Not for me, babe."

"Okay, gotcha." I start packing up the basket stuff. *This is not a date,* I remind myself. But he did kiss me. Maybe he can be my bodyguard with benefits. Just for the weekend.

I pause with the champagne in hand and consider opening it, but it's a little early for drinking. Don't want to go to the reception tipsy.

"Sadie," Deke murmurs.

"Yes?" I answer but don't look at him.

"The dream with the white picket fence and kids, it's not for me."

I frown because he sounds sad again. I'm about to ask *why not* when the phone by the bed rings. I reach over and grab it.

"Sadie! You're here!" the bride shrieks in my ear. There's squealing in the background. Jenn must be with her other bridesmaids, hitting the champagne early.

"Just got in." I sit on the bed.

"Come down!" Jenn says. "We're in room 404."

"Um…" I glance at Deke. The last thing I want to do is leave Deke and go party with the wedding crowd. I feel a little guilty about that—the wedding is the main reason I'm here. "I'm actually a little tired. See you at the reception?"

"Okay, fine. If you and Scott can't drag yourselves

away…" She giggles. Someone in the background shouts something I don't quite hear.

"See you," I quickly make my goodbyes and hang up. Crap. I need to tell Jenn I'm not with Scott anymore. I guess it was too much to hope Scott would tell Geoff, and it'd get back to Jenn.

"Fuuuuudge," I groan and sag backwards onto the bed with my hands covering my face. Is it too much to ask for everything to be called off, so I can stay in the room and seduce Deke? Climb over his walls and get to know him?

Get to know his dick, my ovaries prompt. "Arrrrrghhhh."

"Everything okay?" Deke asks.

"This stuff just stresses me out. I can handle twenty-eight squirming kindergarteners, but formal social affairs remind me too much of suffering through my dad's cocktail parties as a kid. I'd so much rather stay holed up in this room with you."

Deke's eyes glint green. "Yeah?" He stalks toward me with a predatory softness to his tread. Okay, good. We might be on the same page, here.

Yes! Yes! My ovaries are in cheerleading outfits, waving pom poms.

"I might know a way to relieve your stress." His voice is low and suggestive, but I can tell by the way he watches my face for my reaction, he's testing. He's not sure.

"I might be in need of your services." I climb up on the bed on my knees and lift the champagne bottle up like a suggestion.

"Babe." Suddenly I'm flat on my back, my wrists pinned beside my head. Deke takes the champagne bottle from my hand and sets it on the bedside table.

Deke! Deke! Get the D! My ovaries cheer.

"Here's how things are going to go," he tells me. His face

hovers just inches from mine. I can smell his minty breath. "I'm going to strip you naked, tie you to the bed and lick your pussy until you scream. And after you've come all over my tongue about a dozen times, we're going to go down to that party and do whatever it is we're supposed to do. Sounds like a plan?"

I come.

Seriously. That's all it takes. Deke's dark promise makes my pussy clench, a ripple of pleasure running straight to my core.

My teeth actually chatter as I stutter out, "I like the plan."

His smile is feral. "Good girl."

Deke yanks my top off over my head. My breath shudders in, shock and excitement mingling together to turn me into a shivering, quivering ball of nerves.

"Deke…" I actually have nothing more to add to the sentence. I think I'm just saying his name as an honorific. Because he just elevated himself to sex god, and I'm not even naked yet.

Deke uses his middle fingers to hook under each bra strap and tug them down my shoulders. I shimmy my arms through the holes, then hold my breasts when he tugs the cups down. My nipples tingle, my breasts are heavy with desire.

"Mmm. So pretty," Deke rumbles, staring down at my nipples showing between my fingers and thumbs. He covers my hands with his, helping me massage and squeeze my breasts. I'm already wet for him. I squirm beneath his large body, wanting him closer. He spins the band of my bra around and unhooks it, then pulls it out from under me.

"I like the way you're touching yourself, Sadie, but I need you to give me those wrists. He snaps the bra out straight, and I catch his meaning. Another mini orgasm rolls through me as I hold my hands straight up, wrists touching.

"Good girl." He wraps the bra around them, then ties it. I watch him quickly survey the headboard—a fabric-covered, wall-mounted thing—then climb off. In a flash, he has a shoelace out of his boot, and he loops it through my bra-binding, then down behind the bed somewhere. He slides the bed out from the wall, as if it—with me on it—weighs nothing, and in another moment, my wrists get pulled taut above my head as he fastens the shoelace somewhere to the bed.

I'm incredibly turned on by his quick survival skills. Not that tying a woman to a bed is a survival skill, but the Special Forces in him shows, and it's a massive turn-on. Once he has me secure, he takes a long moment drinking me in. His lids droop, and a low rumble sounds in his chest.

I wiggle, trying to entice him back in. His gaze dips to my peaked nipples, and he climbs back over me, lowering his mouth to one. He flicks it with his tongue. Grazes it with his teeth. He palms my breast possessively as he moves his mouth to the other side.

It's delicious. Heaven. I've never been touched by a man like this before. He's so aggressive, yet infinitely more attentive than any lover I've had before.

He grasps the waistband of my pants and tugs them down and off, leaving me in nothing but my provocative panties. I'm so glad I wore them.

"Mmm," he rumbles, sliding a finger under the leg band and tracing it down between my legs. "These are so pretty, Sadie-girl."

A whimper-moan escapes my lips.

"Did you wear these for me?"

My core clenches. "Y-yes."

His eyes glint green, and he draws a sharp breath in through his nostrils, almost like he's trying to steady himself.

"Fuck, Sadie." He squeezes his cock through his jeans. "You have a naughty streak, don't you?"

"Mmm hmm." More clenching. I tug on my bonds, only because I want to touch him, to hurry this thing along.

He runs his knuckle over my panty-clad pussy, making me soak it with arousal.

"Yes," I whimper. "Please."

"Please? That's so fucking sweet." My panties practically fly off my legs.

I shaved a landing strip this morning, and the sight of my trim makes Deke growl. "Was that for me?"

"Yes," I admit.

"Fuck, Sadie." Deke shoves my knees wide and licks me from anus to clit.

I scream and yank at my bonds. It's good—so good! But I've never been licked so intimately. It's embarrassing. And incredible. He penetrates me with his tongue, then parts my nether lips with his tongue, gliding up to my clit again.

"Ohhh, oh!" I moan. "Deke."

"That's right, baby. Say my name when I make you come." He flicks his tongue repeatedly over my clit. It's wonderful and very soon not enough. I jack my hips up to get more.

"Spread your legs wider, baby."

I spread. I spread so wide the ballet lessons of my youth are showing.

"Did you need more?" Somehow he reads my mind. To my utter shock, he gives my pussy several sharp slaps. It doesn't hurt, but it surprises me. "You like having your pussy spanked?"

Oh. My. *Gawd.*

I want to cover my face with my hands. Because I do. I do like it. So freaking much. How does he know that?

"Deke!"

He pat-slaps me a few more times, driving me wild, then lowers his mouth again and licks and sucks his way over all my bits.

"Deke, oh please." I'm desperate for release now—it feels so good.

He finds exactly the right place and sucks hard, and I come, my legs thrashing wildly, my pelvis rolling and undulating as my channel clenches on nothing but air.

"That's one."

My eyes fly wide. Was he serious about giving me multiple orgasms?

I can't deny how hot the scene is—I'm fully naked and tied to the bed, and he's still fully dressed, the guy in charge.

Deke unties my wrists and drops beside me, then rolls us both to our sides. I'm tucked right against him, my small legs tangled with his huge ones.

"Open your legs, baby," he instructs. His hand is already slipping between my legs. *Yes!* My hips tilt to greet him again. He palms me, holding my throbbing sex right in his calloused hand. One finger rubs over my entrance, while his palm grinds against my clit. I instantly soak his finger with natural lubricant, my body eager for his touch. His digits are huge, but he works one into my entrance.

"Deke." I'm caught up in a sudden blaze of heat. His hot breath caresses my ear, and his hips grind into my backside. The rough edge of his long finger catches my clit and sends a shock of pleasure shooting through me. The sensation's so sweet it's almost painful. I cry out and twist my hips, trying to roll away, but Deke is half covering me with his body, and his arm is iron, immovable. And his fingertips gliding through the wet folds of my sex are so soft. His index finger flutters against my clit before he slides lower and inserts two fingers inside me.

Oh! That's what I needed. Penetration. I cry out in pleasure, reaching down to grip his wrist and guide him deeper.

"Fuck, that's it. Take it, Sadie. Take what I give you. Take everything you need."

It's so good. I surrender, allowing the pleasure to build and build, the fire in my belly getting hotter.

"Deke!" My cry sounds alarmed, but if I'm scared, it's only because I've never felt such pleasure.

"Take it, Sadie." Deke's breath rasps in my ear, almost like he's as tortured as I am.

Stars burst behind my eyes. I climax again, gasping in Deke's arms. He doesn't move, doesn't let me move and keeps his palm grinding right against the spot, right there, chasing the aftershocks. My legs scrabble over the covers, and I writhe in his arms, but he holds me fast, making me feel the pleasure in its every exquisite expression. And when it fades, I'm still in Deke's arms, snug and warm.

Totally blissed out.

I'm sticky with sweat. My hair is mussed in the best way—great sex hair. I rise from the bed and glide to the mirror where I can stare at the bright eyed goddess I am. My lips are puffy and parted, my cheeks are flushed orgasm pink.

Deke follows me, a dark shadow hovering at my back. I lean back into his chest, and his arm comes around me, securing me against him. He blew my mind in bed, and he didn't even take off his jeans.

His dark eyes dance in the mirror. His whisper tickles my ear. "Feel better?"

"Oh yes." I turn and put my hands on his chest. "But what about you?"

His eyes seem to change color the way they do sometimes—from brown to a glowing green. With a pained expression, he takes a quick step back from me. "I'm good."

I try not to be disappointed that he's not interested in reciprocation.

This is not a date.

The only thing that confuses me is the size of the bulge in his jeans.

~

Deke

OH FUCK.

I have blue balls the size of my fist. I am fully willing to suffer them to deliver Sadie's satisfaction. Hell, I would take any level of torture to ensure her comfort and ease this weekend.

But it would be so much easier if she didn't seem hurt that I didn't accept her offer to return the favor.

I mean—fuck! If she only knew how much I want that. I would give both nuts to have her small hand wrapped around my cock. Or those sweet, soft lips. But my wolf's getting aggressive.

He seems to be laboring under the impression that Sadie is mine. *Ours.* Whatever.

That means the urge to mark her is starting to fray my control.

My wolf doesn't give a fuck that I can't mark her.

He doesn't care that mating is off-limits for all members of the Shifter Op team but particularly for me. I'm not even remotely safe for a human. I shudder, the thought of actually hurting Sadie if my wolf won control striking real fear into me.

Which makes my wolf snarl protectively.

Oh Fates. Maybe I took on more than I can handle by coming here.

Now I have to go downstairs and interact with a packed room of humans while my wolf is feral as hell. I look out the window, trying to figure out if I have time to get out there and shift.

But no, Sadie needs me. And she is priority one.

I have to get through this insane human tradition of a wedding and keep my wolf in check. And speak in full sentences. And look presentable.

For a guy who has been on the team that toppled entire regimes at the orders of his president, this mission should be a piece of cake. Why does it feel like the most difficult op I've ever been on?

Because I've never cared so much about an op as I do this one.

That's what Sadie does to me.

When it's about danger, about eliminating enemies, I have it covered. Even when I lose control of my wolf, he's still always on point. The job gets done, even if it's bloodier than expected. But in this case, my wolf could hurt Sadie if I lost control, and he marked her. He could even kill her. Humans are fragile creatures. One slice of an artery, and she would—

Fuck, I can't even think about it.

And then there's the issue of the ex. I think I have myself under control, but if my wolf thought she was under threat, even mildly, the results could be deadly.

I clear my throat as Sadie flits about the room. "Okay if I use the shower?"

"Yes, of course. Go for it." She flashes me the kind of

smile that lights up a room, and my heart tumbles off the cliff into Sadieland.

I make myself move, getting into the bathroom and stripping off my clothes. I'll feel better once I've rubbed one out thinking about my beautiful—

No, not mine.

She's not my beautiful anything.

She's a mission. A mission I *will not* fuck up.

I turn the water to completely cold and step under the icy spray. Anything to subdue this raging lust licking at my ears. It doesn't make a dent in the inferno that's my body. I bring my fingers—the ones still covered in her scent—to my nose and inhale deeply. My cock juts out and bobs, and I grip it firmly, jerking myself off remembering the incredible sound she made when I brought her to orgasm.

Sweet Sadie.

My beautiful human.

No, not—

Mine, my wolf rages.

And I let him. Just for the moment. Because the lights are already dancing behind my eyes, and my thighs are already starting to shake. I bottle up the roar rocketing from my throat and come all over the expensive tile walls.

And dammit, I only feel marginally relieved.

The need for Sadie Diaz is consuming me.

CHAPTER 9

adie

I WEAR a dress and heels to the party. Once I've tamed my hair and put on my pearls, I look more presentable, but my cheeks still have that orgasm flush. Deke wears a fresh white t-shirt and a nice pair of black jeans. He shrugs a short-sleeved button down over the t-shirt, which he leaves untucked. I think this is his version of dressing up. With his huge size and tattoos, he still manages to look every bit as dangerous as he does in his leather. I'm not complaining. Deke looks like James Dean's wilder, more dangerous brother, and it does things to me. My nipples are hard under my dress bodice, so I add a fancy cardigan for good measure.

He gets a few double takes when we walk into the party from the middle-aged members of Geoff and Jenn's family. I ignore the raised eyebrows and head to the corner where the bride holds court.

"Sadie!" Jenn cries, throwing out her arms. The champagne glass in her hand tilts, but it's more than half empty.

"You're glowing," her sister Brigit gasps. The rest of the half tipsy bridesmaid posse turns to look.

"So are you," I say to Jenn and lean in to hug her. We pull away and air kiss. "You look so beautiful."

"So do you!" Jenn squeals. She has a giant rock on her finger, blinding with diamonds. I ooh and ahh over the engagement ring for the appropriate amount of time. It cost more than her Jeep Wrangler.

"And who are you?" Laura, Jenn's older cousin, asks, eyeing Deke. Laura's not a bridesmaid, but from the admiring way she's looking at Deke, she appreciates his broad shoulders as much as I do.

"Oh." I step back and put my hand on Deke's arm, claiming him. "Ladies, this is Deke. He's my plus one for the weekend." I rehearsed this in my head. He's not a boyfriend, he's not a friend, he's not a partner. But "plus one" gets the message across.

"Hi, Deke," the women chorus and exchange knowing looks.

Brigit elbows me, waggling her eyebrows approvingly.

Jenn clears her throat. "Champagne?"

I take a glass, and Deke waves it away.

"Congratulations," he says gruffly to Jenn, and she flushes happily.

"Thank you. How did you meet Sadie?"

I open my mouth, feeling flustered. Before I blurt out something random, Deke puts a hand in the small of my back, supporting me.

"Met in Taos, at the plaza. Fate threw us together," he answers. He looks around as if daring anyone to contradict him. "It was meant to be."

The bridesmaids all swoon.

Something squeezes in my chest. The wish that it was all true and not a fabrication.

"That's so wonderful." Brigit winks at me. "Wow," she mouths. I nod back and sip my champagne serenely while Deke stands behind me, my strong, silent back-up.

Jenn pulls me aside the first chance she gets. "Sadie, I'm so sorry. I thought you were still with Scott."

"No, it's okay. We broke up a while back. I didn't want to dump on you while you were planning the wedding," I say. "I'm sorry, I guess I hoped Geoff would tell you."

"Oh, girl, you're fine. I didn't mean to assume you were with Scott. I paired you off for the whole ceremony. Oh no," her hand flies to her mouth. "Are you guys in the same room?"

"No, I called the hotel and got my own room," I assure her. "It's fine. Don't worry about me. This is your big weekend."

"I know!" she squeals and throws up her arms. The diamond glint on her finger catches her eye, and she holds out her hand to gaze adoringly at her ring.

I try not to worry about the mixed messages of Scott walking me down the aisle. But then I glance at Deke, and I hardly care.

A few feet away, the flock of bridesmaids shriek with laughter. I look over and Deke's there, his tall form towering over the giddy women. His eyes are on me not them. Like he's ready to jump in and protect me in case Jenn suddenly assaults me or something. He nods at me, and I smile back, feeling warm inside.

Deke's here. It'll be fine.

Deke

I GET a whiff of Douchebag Cologne and stifle a cough.

I walk away from the tipsy women without a word. One of them calls, "Come back soon" to my back. As if I would ever look at another woman when I have Sadie.

I sidle up to Sadie and hook my arm around her. "Missed ya, babe," I mutter and the human she's talking to—the bride—gives me a big grin.

"Aww, you too," Sadie says.

"You two are so cute together," the bride sighs. "Which reminds me, I should go see what my guy is up to. See you at dinner?"

"Yes," Sadie agrees, and I keep my expression blank. I guess we have to eat sometime, but my wolf is already on edge in this confined place. There are too many people here. Too much noise. My wolf wants me to drag Sadie back upstairs and feast on her pussy instead.

The bride glides away, and Sadie pokes me in the side. "Did you see?"

She means Scott and his new arm candy. "Yep."

"Oh my God," she whispers. "He really is dating someone new."

"Or he's paying for her company."

Sadie wrinkles her nose. "Really?"

"Yeah."

She laughs, and my wolf preens a little. I'm so fucking glad she doesn't give a shit about that guy.

Across the room, Scott sees us and heads right over. I pull Sadie closer. "What's up with her lips? She looks like she's been stung by a bee."

"Those aren't natural. There's some filler involved in

there," Sadie whispers back.

She sips her champagne, surreptitiously watching her ex approach. "I can't believe he dialed a date. At least she's not half his age. Ugh, what did I see in Scott?"

"I have no fuckin' idea."

"Sadie." Scott finally arrives in front of us. I wonder briefly if Sadie would protest if I punched the smirk off his face. "This is Elana."

Elana looks me up and down and angles herself to show off her cleavage as she offers her hand. "Charmed," she says in a husky voice.

I give Elana a nod, and let Sadie shake her hand.

"It's so nice to meet you," Sadie says sweetly. "You probably heard that Scott and I broke up a month ago. I'm so glad he's found someone."

"Your loss, my gain," Elana says.

"Definitely." Sadie looks relieved. "Just to warn you, the bride thought Scott and I were still together, so we're partnered during the wedding. But Scott is all yours." Sadie puts up her hands in Scott's direction like she's pushing him away. "I don't want him *at all.*"

"Got it," Elana says.

"Good! We can all be adults about this. I don't want things to be awkward."

"Oh, I think we can all get along," Elana winks at me.

Sadie notices and angles in closer to me. I fucking love it. She's claiming me. She may not seem like an alpha female, but she has the potential.

"Whatever makes things easy for *Sadie,*" I say with extra emphasis on her name. "She's my priority."

"Aww that's so sweet," Elana says and turns to Sadie. "Looks like you got a good one."

"I did. Hey, did you want some champagne?" Sadie waves Brigit over to get Elana a glass.

"Absolutely." Elana lights up. "Would love a glass."

Scott stands by with a half grimace on his face. If he hoped for a catfight between Sadie and Elana, he's SOL.

"To weddings," Sadie and Elana toast and clink glasses.

"How is everybody doing?" An overly perfumed woman sails over and inserts herself into our group. Beside me, Sadie stiffens.

"Sadie, is that you?" The woman is middle aged with frosted blonde hair. She leans in to invite Sadie to give her a kiss on the cheek and a wave of her intense perfume nearly knocks me out. I duck my head and half turn, wanting to bury my face in Sadie's hair, so I can draw a clean breath. My wolf whimpers.

"Mrs. Atkins," Sadie says politely. She kisses the woman on the cheek and retreats, reaching out to me. I grab her hand, and she squeezes it.

"Oh call me Lacy, you're practically family. And Scott, there you are," Lacy beckons and gets a cheek kiss from him too. "And who is this?" She peers first at Elana, then me.

"Lacy, this is Deke. He's my date for the weekend," Sadie says. "Deke, this is Jenn's mom."

Scott quickly follows up, introducing his date.

Lacy frowns. "Oh are you two not together anymore? Shame on you, Sadie, letting our Scott get away!" She pokes Scott in the chest. "I was going to make sure you had a front place for the bouquet toss. I thought you two would be next."

Sadie is wincing. Lacy's voice is as loud as her perfume, so other guests are turning. I blink to keep my eyes from watering.

"What's this now?" A tall, thin man with a bored expression permanently stapled to his face arrives. He halts next to

Lacy, who turns to inform him, "You remember Scott and Sadie, George? These are their dates."

The man turns to me. "And what do you do?"

"Security." I keep my hand holding Sadie's. Not that this guy's offering to shake.

"You're Sadie's bodyguard?" The man manages to look down his nose at both of us, even though he's shorter than me.

"No, although he could be," Sadie fake laughs. I can smell her tension. "He was in the military, and now he owns a security business."

"Ah, a start up," the man says dismissively.

I shrug. "If multi-million dollar government contracts are for start-ups."

The guy's eyes bulge.

"Got thirty employees, worldwide." I hate giving out information, but this is for Sadie. No one is going to make her feel small. In this stupid dick measuring contest, size matters. The size of our company.

George considers me with a sudden new-found respect.

"Thirty employees? I didn't know that," Sadie says, looking up at me, impressed.

Lacy's eyes narrow. "You didn't?"

"We just met." Sadie sounds defensive, and I wish I could tell her to relax. These people don't matter.

"Does your father know about this?" George asks Sadie, and she presses her lips together. I don't know why the comment disturbs Sadie, but I make a note to find out. And to give George's info to the hackers on payroll, to see if he's hiding anything. That way, if George upsets Sadie again, I can crush him.

"Mr. Diaz and I still have lunch monthly," Scott butts in. "He's given me invaluable insight on the Denson project." He and George start talking about permits and zoning, while the rest of us stand awkwardly by.

"Have you looked at the itinerary?" Sadie asks Lacy, in an attempt to change the subject. "There's all sorts of fun stuff available at the resort. There's a zip line and everything!"

Elana looks bored. Lacy turns to me, "I don't suppose you would like to join me for morning yoga? It's outdoors on the lower deck."

Whoa. Didn't see that coming. The cougar's on the prowl.

"Oh, I'm not sure that's Deke's thing," Sadie says, trying to save me. I squeeze her hand.

"If Sadie wants to go, I'd be honored to join."

"Are you sure?" Lacy asks in a way I know this is a test. "It's pretty early in the morning."

I shrug, "Can't be worse than basic training."

"Ah yes, you were military. What branch?"

"Army, ma'am," I say. "Special forces."

"Well, you know he has discipline," she says to Sadie with an appreciative lilt to her voice.

Yeah. Barely enough discipline to keep from throwing her over my shoulder and carrying her up to our room.

"And I do love a man in uniform." Lacy straightens slightly in a way that pushes out her boobs. "Nice to meet you, Deke. Look forward to seeing you tomorrow morning."

"All right, everybody," Brigit calls from the front of the room. "Can I get everyone's attention? The dining hall is ready to seat our party."

People start to stream out of the room, but Sadie and I hold back. I don't show it, but I'm edgy as hell. The last place I want to go is in even tighter quarters with these people. This is the most I've spoken to humans in ages, and my wolf desperately wants to either fuck or fight to relieve the tension.

"Oh my God," Sadie mutters. "That was awful. I'm so sorry."

"Babe." She's so fucking sweet. I don't want her to worry about me. I just want her to stop worrying completely.

As we start to follow the others heading to the dining room, she tugs me down a side corridor. It's dimly lit with fancy sconces that must be for decoration because they do a shit job of actually lighting anything.

"Are you okay? I know you don't like crowds."

I go still. "You noticed that?" Fuck, I'm not doing as good a job on this mission as I'd hoped.

She nods, her warm brown eyes studying my face with so much compassion. "Is it PTSD?" she asks softly.

I rub a hand over my face. "Yeah." Let's go with that. I hate lying, but telling Sadie I'm a werewolf who can't keep his animal in check obviously isn't going to happen.

She tests a door and pushes it open. It's a meeting room, unlit and empty. "Come here." She tugs me inside.

"I'm okay, babe." I hate that she's worrying over me now. I'm supposed to be doing her the favors. But then she unbuttons my jeans and sudden heat explodes below my waist.

"Let me help ease the tension." She lowers to her knees, and I lose all rational thought. "It's the least I can do after what you did for me."

"Sadie," I choke, but my hand's already in her dark, thick hair. I'm incapable of telling her she doesn't have to do this. Refusing the pleasure she's so generously offering.

She frees my length and smiles up at me as she fists it. I've never seen such a beautiful sight in my life.

She takes her time, swirling her tongue around the head of my cock. My back hits the wall behind me with a thud. My legs start shaking. Heat flares everywhere.

Miraculously, I don't feel that mindless aggression I

sensed before, when I was on top of her. That feeling like my canines were about to descend to mark her forever as mine. My wolf seems willing to just receive.

The entire moment is a gift.

My heart hammers under the new shirt I bought for this weekend. My breath rasps in and out as my cock stretches and arcs, harder than marble under her tongue. She lifts her warm brown gaze to mine as her soft lips part to take me into her mouth.

I choke on a groan. My fist in her hair tightens. "Oh fates, Sadie. That's so nice."

She withdraws then takes me deeper. Repeats the action. My thighs shake harder. I don't help or guide her head, I just let her drive, humbled by her sweetness. This human is everything.

Kind, beautiful, adorably funny. Even though being with her is a constant torture, I also haven't felt this light in years. Possibly not since I joined the Army ages ago. I stroke her cheek with my thumb as she bobs her head over my cock and back, taking me into the pocket of her cheek in short, delicious pumps. Her velvety tongue swirls underneath my dick each time she brings me deep, her cheeks hollow each time she sucks hard on her way back out.

I'm dying of ecstasy.

I want it to last all night, but I already need to come.

I lean my head back against the wall and close my eyes to stall, to savor a little more of this intense, hedonistic pleasure.

Sadie keeps working my cock like a champ. The kindergarten teacher has transformed into a pornstar, and I want to throw her on her back and—

No.

No, not that.

I can't claim her.

I can't claim her, but I will definitely get my mouth on her and return this favor before the night is through. I will make her scream so loud the resort walls shake and the lights shatter.

"Sadie," I choke. The fuse she lit on my orgasm is burning too fast. Heat spikes at my tailbone. My balls draw up tight. "Sadie, I'm going to come," I warn her in a guttural rasp.

She doesn't stop. Sadie goes faster, sucks harder, her beautiful doe eyes lifted to mine like she wants to see my face when I come undone. I don't mean to, but the leash on my control snaps. I grasp her head with both hands and fuck her mouth, once, twice, three times. On the fourth, I come down her throat.

She holds still for it.

Swallows.

Sweet Sadie swallows. Unbelievable.

"I'm sorry," I croak, realizing how disrespectful I've been. I release her head abruptly, but she doesn't jerk away. She sucks off my cock, cleaning me and swallowing again, her eyes dancing with her own pleasure at what she's done.

I stroke her face, instinctively massage her ears, forgetting she's not a she-wolf. "Fates," I breathe. "That was incredible, Sadie."

"Was it?" She wipes her mouth as I tuck my dick away, and I help her stand.

"You're incredible." I can't stop myself from saying every thought that arrives in my brain. "Best blowjob of my life."

"I doubt that." Her laugh is husky and pleased.

"Swear to fate."

"To fate?" She cocks her head, her curious gaze traveling over my face.

Whoops.

I tug her body up against mine. "I mean to God." I shrug. "Fate is a word my family used to use." I can't lie to her any more. "My parents are nature-loving hippies in Vermont," I find myself telling her, even though I haven't spoken about my parents in ages. "Pacifists. They hated that I joined the Army."

"Thank you for your service," she murmurs.

"Fuck, you're sweet." I stroke the lovely line of her cheek with my thumb and lower my head for a kiss. My lips brush across hers lightly. My aggression is gone, relieved by the incredible orgasm.

She rises on her toes to kiss me back.

The aggression returns. I cup the back of her head to hold her in place, my lips slanting over hers with more insistence. I lick into her mouth. Claim it.

Voices sound from the hallway—two guests talking about the wedding as they pass.

Sadie pulls back with a smile. "We should get in there."

"Yeah." I don't want to move. "I'd rather take you upstairs and return the favor."

She presses her body against mine. "You being my date is your favor," she reminds me in the sexiest voice I've ever heard. "This was my payback."

"All right then." I duck my head to murmur in her ear, "But I'm gonna need one more thing."

"What is it?"

"Take off your panties."

Her eyes dilate, and the scent of her arousal fills my nostrils. "What? Here?"

"Uh huh. I want you bare and thinking about my mouth on your sex all night long. Anticipating what you're gonna get when I bring you back to that room."

A shiver runs through her, and her delicious scent

increases. She glances toward the door to the hall. We can hear more guests laughing and talking beyond the hall, but the sound's receding like they're heading away. My shifter hearing will alert me of anyone who might interrupt us. I won't let anyone catch us, but Sadie doesn't know that, and I don't tell her. The thrill is half the fun.

"Better make it fast. Someone might come looking for us," I tease.

"Oh God." She scrambles out of her panties. I get a flash of bare leg and then her skirt falls back in place. But her cheeks are bright pink, the same color as her panties.

I hold out my hand for them. After a second of hesitation she drops the tiny scrap of silky lace into my big palm. My dick throbs. I close my fist, fighting the urge to do more.

"Deke?" She looks up at me so trusting.

I shove her panties in my pocket. "Let's go, babe." I claim her hand and tug her back towards the party.

"Oh my God," she whispers. As we walk down the hall she keeps turning her head to check her backside as if she's afraid her dress is riding up the back.

"Don't worry about it," I stop just before we exit the hall and smooth a hand down her bottom under the pretense of stroking her skirt. "I won't let you moon anybody." My wolf would happily take out any man who's seen Sadie naked. I'll be on guard the whole evening, just to make sure no one even gets close.

No one touches Sadie, no one but me.

I palm her ass, bare beneath the dress's fabric, and squeeze.

"Oh God," Sadie says again.

"Be a good girl," I tell her. "And later I'll give you your reward."

CHAPTER 10

adie

I DON'T KNOW how I get through dinner. I feel like there's a giant neon sign above my head. *SADIE DIAZ IS NOT WEARING PANTIES.*

Deke's the only one who knows. And the longer dinner and drinks stretch on, the more he's dying to do something about it, I can tell.

It's the first time in my life I've felt sexual power. Seeing him come undone with the blowjob started it. Now I'm receiving heated looks and low growls. Next time I lean in to laugh at something a guest beyond us said, I brush my breasts against his arm. His *hard muscled* arm.

The joke's on me, though, because my nipples bead up beneath my dress.

Next I rub my foot against his long leg. He moves it, planting it in front of me. Then he puts his hand on my knee, and slowly slides his fingers up my thigh. My belly shudders in on a gasp. I'm afraid I'll cry out if he reaches the apex, so I grasp his wrist just in time. His hand is so big, his long fingers are mere inches away from my pussy. My bare naked pussy.

My breath leaves and sucks in again. I'm feverish.

Beside me, Deke's eyebrow flicks slightly, but other than that, he gives no sign that he was about to finger me right here, right now, right at dinner. Meanwhile, I'm a squirming mess. Unlike Deke, I don't have a Sexy Seduction Stealth Mode.

"Are you okay, Sadie?" Brigit asks from across the table. "You look a little overheated."

"Fine," I gurgle and hold up my glass. "Just too much champagne. I might go get some water."

"You have water right there," Elana points to my glass.

"Oh right," I grab it and rise. "I meant air. I need air," I announce to everyone and scoot away from the table. I grab my cardigan, which I took off and hung on the back of my chair for dinner. I also make sure to hold my skirt down as I head out to the balcony, just in case it rides up.

The night has a bite to it, and it's perfect. My heels clatter on the wood. I'm not dressed to stay out here long, but right now the chilly air and star-studded sky are what I need. I take a deep breath and another.

Then a shadow falls alongside me. Somehow Deke's followed me without me hearing. His big boots make no sound on the wooden deck. Total Stealth Mode.

I check, but no one back inside noticed he's slipped out here with me. They're sitting at the restaurant table, talking and laughing with each other.

"You," I accuse.

"Me." He backs me up to the balcony ledge, where he bends me back and kisses me.

Heat rolls through my body, heady and potent, like I've drunk a draught of whiskey. The stars are spinning overhead when I pull away to gasp, "Deke. Someone might see."

"Let 'em see," he growls. The rough stubble on his jaw scrapes my cheek. "Isn't that why I'm here? To put on a show?"

I feel a flash of disappointment. Right. This isn't a real date.

Only, damn—it was feeling so real. Is this all fake to him?

"You're right," I answer, acting as calm as I can. "Better kiss me again."

"Oh, I'm going to do more than that."

And he draws me deeper into the shadows. We move along the back deck, down the stairs and to a hidden corner that overlooks a stunning view of the range. On Saturday, the bride will get married with these mountains as a backdrop. But tonight they're dark and somnolent giants, their rocky shoulders half blanketed with pine trees.

I follow Deke because he has a plan, but I stop a moment to take in the view.

"It's beautiful out here," I whisper. And shiver because what little heat I brought outside with me has dissipated, and I'm only wearing a cardigan against the chill.

Deke shrugs out of his button-down and tucks it around me, ignoring my protests that he'll be cold. His white t-shirt shines in the darkness. He pulls me against his large chest.

"We should go back in," I say, even though I'm warm and cozy now, swaddled in his shirt and arms. "You're going to freeze."

He chuckles, as if the idea of him being cold is a joke. "You'll keep me warm," he says and turns me back to face the mountains. His arms slide around me, and I lean back against his front.

"Not that warm. I'm in a dress and *no panties*," I remind him. Judging by the giant hard-on poking my butt, he hasn't forgotten the *no panties* part.

"Mmmm." He nuzzles my neck. "You must be ready for your reward." His lips brush my ear. "Put your hands on the railing."

I lean forward to obey.

He flips up my skirt. Cold air gusts over my bare butt, and my entire body breaks out into goosebumps. His fingers caress my bottom, gliding over the chilled skin, exploring.

I shift from foot to foot, still holding position, aroused and excited but nervous. "Someone could come find us," I whisper over my shoulder.

"I won't let anyone see you," he promises. His big hands cover my butt cheeks, squeezing and offering a little heat. "Besides, no one cares."

"I guarantee Scott cares," I say and immediately curse myself for bringing up Scott.

"Gonna make you forget him," Deke says, and it sounds like a vow.

He brushes his fingertip between my legs.

"Already forgotten."

He presses me forward, and now I'm leaning on the railing while he fondles my backside. He reaches under to find and stroke my labia with soft fingers. I rise to tiptoe, but his other hand holds my hips steady, so I can't get away. I'm bent over with my butt sticking out and on display, exposed and offered up to this bad boy.

"You're turning me into a bad girl," I breathe.

His fingers pause. "I don't think so. I think you've always been bad."

He pulls his hand out from between my legs to give my butt a slap. I gasp. The sound seems to reverberate in the still air. My heart stutters, and I freeze, listening hard as if the sound will echo off the mountains. But it doesn't, and Deke rewards my bravery with more pussy rubbing.

"You sucked my cock like a porn star. I think you have a real naughty streak." His fingers continue to thrum between my folds, alternating with a few hard smacks that seem to jolt arousal through me. Then he goes back to stroking me to orgasm.

I go on tiptoe, grinding down onto his fingers, with the hazy light of the Milky Way rippling overhead, flung between the mountains and the opposite horizon like a diamond studded scarf. Cold fingers of wind caress my face, but I'm snuggled deep into Deke's shirt and his scent where the chill can't touch me.

"That's it, grind down," Deke orders, thumbing my clit as he slips a thick finger inside me. "Take your pleasure, baby, take it."

I twist my hips, searching for the right angle, for more stimulation.

"Fuck," Deke mutters. "Gotta taste you." He drops to his knees behind me and spreads my legs wider and puts his mouth on me. His stubble scratches up my inner thighs as his tongue searches for my secret folds. I'm tipped to my front, nails digging into the wood, pushing my bottom back as I try to ride his face. It's not the best angle, it's a bit ridiculous, and I don't care.

He growls and buries his face between my legs, holding my hips, half lifting me off the ground. "Fuck," he says again and turns me to face him, propping me on the top of the deck railing at the same time. And then his dark head is between my legs again, my skirt flung up over my belly and bunching around my hips. My hands grip the railing, but Deke's got me, somehow steading my legs as he eats me out. My thighs are propped over his big shoulders, his tongue is *right there,* and *oh fudge*....

I come, pleasure crashing down and making me bend double over his head. He shakes his head, scratching the sensitive skin of my inner thighs with his bristled cheeks before lapping at my pussy again. The chafing sensation is just this side of painful, and my abs clench with another wave of pleasure. And then I'm falling, wrung out, toppling over, totally boneless. Deke catches me, of course, and lifts me in his arms.

I hear footsteps and loud voices on the upper deck, but I'm too orgasm-drunk to care. I let my head loll against his shoulder as Deke carries me up the deck stairs swiftly and towards a side entrance back into the resort.

I hear a shocked giggle from someone who sees us, but I don't know who it is.

"Too much champagne," Deke tosses the explanation over his shoulder. I wave goodbye in whoever-it-is' general direction and laugh against Deke's t-shirt as he carries me over the threshold like a bride.

Deke

I HAVE a hard time not growling at every person we pass on the way to the room. My wolf is damn pleased that I got her off, but the need to claim her is even stronger, especially with all the people around.

She tucks her head against my neck as I carry her, her breath even and smooth. She must be sleepy and relaxed from her orgasm.

Deposit the package and get out.

The thought forms in Rafe's alpha bark.

Discipline is the only thing keeping us from moon madness.

I open the door to our room and tip Sadie down to her feet, giving her ass a light slap. "I need to get some fresh air," I tell her.

She blinks at me, surprise and a touch of hurt flickering over her expression. "We were just outside."

"I know. I need to go for a run. It's, ah, the PTSD. I get restless, and it helps me sleep."

Fuck, I feel like the biggest asshole for lying to her.

Sympathy sweeps over her features, and she reaches up to touch my face. I catch her hand and bring it to my lips before I can help myself. Her expression softens even more. "Is it okay with you? You're okay here?"

"Yes, of course. I understand."

Thank fuck. I change into a pair of gym shorts that I'd planned on sleeping in, but I don't have running shoes, which is a bit suspicious. I settle for kicking off my shoes.

Sadie emerges from the bathroom where she washed her face and brushed her teeth. Her eyes fly wide when she sees my running attire. "Oh! Are you one of those barefoot runners?"

I didn't know there was such a thing, but I nod. It's not a lie.

"Wow. That's incredible," she breathes. "I've heard of it, and I understand the theory behind it, but it boggles my mind."

Since I have no clue about the theories behind it, I move in and drop a light kiss on her forehead. "Don't wait up."

"Oh! Um, okay."

I head for the door.

"You can sleep in the bed with me when you get back." She sounds almost shy as she offers.

"Babe." I don't want to tell her no, but sleeping beside her is definitely not an option. Not if I want to keep her safe from me.

In fact, I don't plan to come back to this room until the night is mostly over, and I've run myself into the ground.

I leave before she tempts me into staying longer and make a beeline for outside. I find a hiking trail and follow it away from the resort until it's safe to strip and shift.

And then I take off up the mountain, running from Sadie. Running from myself.

Running until I'm sure it's safe to come back.

CHAPTER 11

adie

I WAKE up in a warm bed. It's morning already, and Deke's side of the bed is empty. On his pillow there's a note that reads "Gone for another run. Meet you at yoga."

I had hoped for a continuation of our sexual escapades last night, but I didn't hear Deke come back to the room.

Too bad.

I hop up and get ready for yoga. When I pull the curtains, the gorgeous view greets me. I feel great, sparkly with energy and a good night's sleep. I slept better last night than I have in weeks. Maybe we didn't get to fool around in bed again, but it's wonderful to have Deke here.

Today is going to be a good day. First I have to get through yoga, but then we have free time before the rehearsal dinner tonight. Maybe I can convince Deke to spend it with me in bed.

A half an hour later, I'm outside with the bride and the

rest of the ladies assembled on the front deck. I blush when I see the corner where Deke and I spent time last night. I have fond memories of that corner.

"Hey, Sadie," Brigit greets me when I roll out a mat next to hers. She's in full makeup and Lululemon from head to toe. Most of the women wear the same. "Sleep well?"

"Yep. All this mountain air," I say.

"You going to hike later? April and I went out early this morning. It was really nice."

"Deke already went for a run," I say. "He was up before I got up."

"Oh, is he a morning person?"

"Um, yes." I guess. I actually have no idea. It's not like Deke and I are actually dating.

"Ask him if he saw any wildlife. We saw a bunch of hawks and April thinks she saw a wolf."

"It was a giant wolf," April insists from her mat on the other side of Brigit. "I didn't see it clearly, but I saw something. It had a big tail."

"Probably a large coyote." Brigit sounds skeptical, and April sticks her tongue out at her cousin.

"I bet there are tons of wolves in this area," I say.

"Yeah, but no way one would come so close to the resort," Brigit slips in the last word before the instructor starts the class.

"Isn't Deke supposed to be here?" Brigit whispers. Jenn and her mom, Lacy, turn from their spots to wave at me.

"Whoa," one of the women murmurs appreciatively. I turn to look to the deck stairs, where Deke has appeared. He's already barefoot for some reason, and for yoga attire, he's thrown on a pair of loose sweats. But it doesn't matter because he's not wearing anything else. He's bare chested, with his white t-shirt draped over his broad shoulders, and every muscle on his chest stands out in beautiful relief. He must have gotten hot on his run.

"Sorry, I'm late," he mutters to the yoga instructor, who looks like she'd like to ditch our class to do a private couple's yoga session with Deke. There's a chorus of murmurs from the assembled ladies as Deke prowls among us. Two ladies rush to grab a mat for him. There's not much room left, so after nodding in my direction, Deke arranges himself next to the instructor. She eventually finds her voice and starts the class, and we all pretend to follow along, though really everyone is watching Deke, who still hasn't put his shirt back on. There are heaters set up on the deck, but it's still not that warm, but Deke must be hot blooded, and thank St. Theresa —or whomever is the patron saint of lady boners—for that.

Had I known what Deke was hiding under his James Dean t-shirts and leather jackets, I'd rid the world of every Deke-sized article of clothing, just so he'd go around nude. Each yoga position makes his muscles pop. But his body is smooth and sleek and not stiff like a gym bound body builder. It's a work of art, and this morning we are all Sister Wendy, the late nun/art critic. Especially when Deke does Warrior II pose, feet planted and arms outstretched. With the mountain range in the background, he looks like a model for athleisure wear.

Jenn swivels her head to me and mouths "Wow." Even her mom looks impressed.

When the class ends, Deke comes right to my side and drops a kiss on my lips, playing the dutiful boyfriend perfectly.

"Great work," I whisper to him, and he cocks a curious eyebrow at me. "I'll tell you later." I pat his chest and then keep petting it because it's so yummy.

"You guys want to join us in the hot tub?" Jenn asks.

"We're all headed there." She drops her voice to add, "Although Scott might be there. He asked me what you were up to today."

I fake a grimace. "Then I'll pass." The truth is, I could care less about Scott, but I know the group socializing isn't Deke's thing, and I'm grateful for an excuse to bow out. I feel like a disloyal bridesmaid, but I'd much rather spend time with Deke than the wedding party today.

"You guys have plans for the day?" Lacy pops her nosy head into our circle.

"Uhhhh," I search my brain for something that involves Deke and I and a low chance of running into Scott.

"I've got some ideas," Deke says, slinging an arm around me.

"I'll leave it up to you then," I lean into him, feeling relief. "Deke's such a romantic, he plans the best dates," I announce to the group. Jenn and Brigit grin. "But first, brunch. I'm starving."

"Maybe we can go for a hike," I whisper to Deke as we head to the restaurant, trying to let him off the hook. "Whatever, I don't care. I'm fine with ditching the crowd—I know you're not into it."

"I've got it covered," he answers, pulling out his phone. He walks me through the buffet line and settles me at a corner table then excuses himself to make a call.

Unfortunately, that leaves me open to a line of attack.

"Is this seat taken?" Lacy and Jenn's stepdad George sits down before I can say no. They wave over another couple, Jim and John, Lacy's brother and his husband. By the time Deke gets back, the table is full.

Sorry, I mouth. He squeezes my shoulder and takes his seat, keeping a reassuring hand on me.

"Oh, Sadie, you're not going to eat those," Lacy scolds

me before I can put a forkful of pancakes into my mouth. Memories of years of playdates at Jenn's house growing up with her mom imposing all her body issues on the two of us come flooding back. "So many carbs." She shudders. "But I suppose you can work it off later. Those kindergarteners keep you on your toes, I'm sure."

I set down my fork with a sigh.

"Are you still enjoying teaching?"

"Yes, I love it," I insist. Lacy is like the female version of my dad. There's just no escaping all the judgements.

"I know your father hoped you'd go into law like him. At least you can find a husband to support you." She pats my hand.

I grimace-smile at my plate and saw my breakfast sausage into tiny pieces. It's just like a dinner with my dad, where I cut up my food, unable to put it in my stomach. My body is tense, ready for fight or flight as if Lacy's busybody questions are a threat.

George turns to Deke. "And where did you go to school?"

"Lakewood High," Deke says without missing a beat.

"No, I meant college."

"Didn't go to college. Joined the Army when I turned eighteen. It was not long after 9-11, and I wanted to serve my country. Would've joined earlier if I could've."

Swoon. Deke is total hero material.

He's so different from men like George, my dad and Scott, who are just focused on themselves. Getting ahead. Making appearances.

Deke takes a huge bite of steak. He has no trouble eating.

"Hmmm," George says. "Any thoughts on getting your degree now?"

"Don't need it. Army taught me what I needed to know.

Rest I can learn on my own." Deke bares his teeth, and George's fork clatters to the table.

"You were special ops, right?" I ask, fascinated. I know I shouldn't reveal how little I know about Deke. Lacy is collecting tidbits of information like a squirrel collects acorns. I'm sure the first time she bumps into my dad back in Taos, she'll drag all the dirt she picked up out to shame him.

"Special ops in the Army? Night Stalkers?" George asks.

"Something like that," Deke says.

It's too much for me. Deke isn't even a real date. He definitely doesn't deserve the third degree from these people who aren't even related to me.

"Okay, that's enough of grilling my date," I tell them, using my kind but firm teacher voice.

Lacy looks shocked. I never talk back. At least, I never have before.

I have to say, it feels great. Liberating. With Deke backing me up, it's easy to be strong.

"Almost finished, babe?" Deke nudges me.

"Yes." I lay down my utensils, more than ready to be done.

"Going somewhere?" George asks. "A hike perhaps?"

"Not a hike," Deke says. "Got something special planned for Sadie." He rises, and I do, too.

"It's a surprise for me too," I explain to the table as Deke grabs my jacket and helps me into it. "But I guess I need my jacket."

"Gotta bundle up," Deke agrees. "Ride's almost here."

And then I hear it. The rhythmic sound of chopper blades. A helicopter is approaching, flying up to the resort.

"What's that?" Diners turn in their seats.

"Oh my goodness," Lacy says as the army green helicopter hovers over the huge lawn. "Is there some sort of military exercise?"

"Nope. That's our ride," Deke announces. "Called in a favor."

"Is that even legal?" George frowning, looking over his glasses. The helicopter has landed, but the big rotors still turn, ready to lift off at any moment.

"Come on," Deke holds out his hand. I grab it, and we head out the doors and then run over the lawn, bent over to the chopper.

"I can't believe this," I shout. The sound's immediately whipped away by the roar of the rotors.

The pilot in the front seat is a giant guy with a bushy brown beard. He's got muscles bigger than Deke, which I didn't think was possible.

"This is Teddy," Deke shouts right in my ear, so I can hear him over the sound of the chopper.

"Nice to meet you!" I shout, and Teddy grins at me. Even though it's cold, Teddy isn't wearing a jacket, just old fatigue pants and an army green t-shirt that shows off his impressive tattoos and biceps. Another bad ass from Deke's world.

Deke lifts me into the chopper and straps me in tight. My hair's blown all crazy over my face, and he takes a moment to stroke it back before fastening goggles and a helmet on my head.

"This is incredible!" I shout. "I can't believe this! Where are we going?" I doubt he can hear me over the roar of the helicopter blades.

Instead of answering, he boops my nose and climbs past me to his own seat. Once he's strapped in, he gives a signal to Teddy, and the helicopter lifts off the lawn. I grab the sides of my seat. My stomach swoops as we rocket away, over the resort grounds towards the range. And then we're flying up the face of the mountain and over it, heading north with the Sangre de Cristos spread under us in stunning vista. And ahead, nothing but blue sky, the eagles and us.

I reach over for Deke, and he grabs my hand. We hold tight to each other as Teddy tips us one way, then the other, giving us both an eagle-eye view of the New Mexico landscape below. The buildings and roads look like child toys, tiny pieces lost in the greater wilderness. The roads give way to miles and miles of patchwork color—the pine trees aglow with their shimmery yellow leaves, in between the green-blue of the spruce and pine. The tops of the tallest mountains are streaked with white snow.

It's so beautiful, I choke up. I squeeze Deke's hand harder, and he squeezes back. The chopper's too loud for us to talk, but we don't need words to share the moment.

Finally, Teddy sets the chopper down on a bare hill top. The grass flattens in a wide circle, and the branches of the surrounding trees wave wildly in the man-made wind.

"This is our stop," Deke shouts. He grabs a picnic basket I didn't notice strapped in the back and comes around to help me out of my seat again. The cold gusts through me, but the fresh mountain air is worth the chill. Teddy touches his forehead with two fingers and flicks them in my direction in silent farewell before lifting the chopper and flying off again.

"He'll be back," Deke says. He puts down the picnic basket and helps me out of my helmet and goggles before stripping off his own.

"This is crazy!" I burst out. I do a spin with my arms flung out like I'm Maria in *Sound of Music*. Green grass on the mountain top, birds chirping, trees all around, the scene is pretty enough to be in a movie. "I can't believe you arranged this!"

Deke lays out the red and white checkered picnic blanket.

"Figured the wedding party can't follow us here."

"So you just rented a helicopter?" I shake my head as I sit on the blanket. "This is unreal."

"Teddy's an old friend. He was into it. He packed all this." Deke sets a picnic basket worthy of Yogi Bear next to me. It's full of sandwiches, bottled ice tea and all sorts of goodies like grapes and cashews and a cheese plate.

"Oh, yum." I get busy setting up our meal while Deke stretches out beside me. "Teddy didn't want to stay for the picnic?"

"Teddy was gonna stick around. His original idea was to serenade us."

"Aww, that's so sweet! You told him no?"

"Teddy plays the bagpipes. I told him *fuck, no.*"

I cover my face and laugh. "This is incredible. My God, Deke, this is the best thing anyone's ever done for me. Thank you so much." I bite my lip. I want to lean down and kiss him, but as soon as our lips touch, I know I'm going to want more. Outdoor sex in October never appealed to me before, but if there was a guarantee that Deke's friend wouldn't come back and get an aerial view of me naked, I'd totally do it.

Deke shakes his head as if he knows my thoughts. "You want to thank me, eat some of this." He hands me the cheese plate. "You barely touched breakfast."

Warmth spreads through me. *He noticed.*

Who is this guy? He's too good to be true.

"Don't have to tell me twice." My stomach growls.

"I told Teddy to pack girly shit. I figured you'd like that stuff."

"What girly shit? Olive tapenade?" I spread the tapenade on a cracker and hold it in front of his mouth. "Open," I order.

He shakes his head but obeys.

"So is Teddy one of your army buddies?" I ask.

"Something like that." Deke says, cagey as always when he's talking about his old career.

"So you could tell me, but then you'd have to kill me," I tease.

His lips quirk. "Something like that."

"And he threw all this together in what, an hour?"

Deke shrugs. "I may have prepped him."

"Operation Save Sadie," I quip, and his cheek curves for a second in a stealth smile.

"What did you do in the military, anyway?" I ask after I've devoured most of the cheese plate. I'm fascinated even though I know he's not going to tell me anything.

"I did whatever the Army told me to do."

I roll my eyes.

"I'll tell you," he says, scooting closer to me on the picnic blanket. "but you got to give me something in return."

"I'm not giving you my panties," I say flatly, and he throws back his head and laughs. The sound warms me from the inside out.

I pop a grape into my mouth and enjoy the rare sight of Happy Deke.

"No," Deke says when he's done laughing. "I was thinking more you tell me what's up between you and your dad."

I bite my lip and look away. "I just never made him happy."

"Is that your job? Make your dad happy?" Just like Deke to slice to the heart of the matter in as few words as possible.

"He thinks so." I toy with a few cashews on the plate. "Ever since my mom left me. My mom didn't want to leave me," I clarify. "She finally got fed up with my dad but didn't have the money to divorce him. So she moved away. He didn't let her take me. She tried, but she couldn't afford the lawyers to fight. And I was just a kid. I didn't get a say. I would've gone with her."

"Sucks, babe," Deke sums it up in his typical Deke manner.

"Yes. Yes, it does." I toss the cashews into the woods for a lucky squirrel.

Deke takes my hand and threads his fingers with mine. "This wedding, these people, this is your dad's sort of scene?"

"Yep. All of it. Jenn and I grew up together. Lacy and George are friends of his."

"You don't need to impress these people."

"I know, I know, but—"

"No. They should be working to impress you."

I let those words settle over me like another warm blanket.

"I felt braver with you beside me," I admit. "I'm a nice person, but I can be a doormat. Having my own bodyguard makes it easier to set boundaries."

Deke's eyes glint green in the sunlight. He cups the back of my neck and yanks my lips to his. I groan and tug him closer, slanting my head to offer my mouth fully up to him. Our tongues tangle, heat rising between us. I want to shrug out of my coat and straddle him. Start something and see where we end up.

But Deke's phone beeps between us. I draw back, feeling dizzy. "You should probably get that."

Deke checks his phone, looks away and swears under his breath.

"What? Is something wrong?"

"Nope. Nothing to worry about, babe. C'mon. Let's pack up before Teddy gets back."

~

Deke

"WHAT THE FUCK ARE YOU THINKING?" The rage in my alpha's voice sets my teeth on edge. After returning to the resort, I excused myself from Sadie's side and headed outside to return Rafe's call. She has no idea how much trouble I'm in. Even if she did, she wouldn't understand. She's human, I'm not.

Another reason we don't belong together.

"We are still trying to sort out the shit that went down in Switzerland, and you decide to take off. I thought you were going for a hunt as a wolf. Burn off that edginess you've had since you met that human. I assumed you were alone, doing what you needed to do. Today I get a call from Teddy Medvedev saying he picked up you and the female in a bird in Santa Fe and took you for a ride."

Fuck. Shoulda known Ted the Med would be in touch with my pack. I didn't ask him to keep things quiet to keep from raising his suspicion.

I duck around the side of the resort building, heading to the forest where I can speak freely.

"Is it true?" Rafe demands. "Are you with Sadie Diaz right now?"

"Yeah. It's true." Frankly, I'm surprised Lance didn't already rat me out. I expected this call at least twenty-four hours ago.

Rafe cusses so loudly I have to hold the phone away from my ringing ears. "What the fuck, Deke? After all I told you, you do the exact opposite. And now I gotta order you to stay away—"

"It's a security mission—not a date." I cut him off before he can finish the order. "She needed a fake date for a wedding to keep Sears off her back. That's it. And I'm not abandoning her now. I made a promise."

Silence. My alpha's so pissed, I can hear his teeth grinding. "This is a bad idea, Adalwulf."

"I know. Fuck, I *know.*"

"It won't end well."

"I can do it." I rub my forehead with a thumb, trying to keep a pleading tone out of my voice. I'd fall to my knees and pray if Fate would hear. "I can keep control."

"You have to. The stakes are too high."

He's right. If I lose control, I risk damaging the most precious person on earth. "I'll be careful."

"That's not good enough." Rafe sighs, but he doesn't order me home.

"I will keep control," I repeat and mean it. I'll do anything—even if I have to drive Sadie away.

"You'd better." Rafe mutters. "You're a danger to her. Get out as soon as you can, before it's too late."

Sadie

How's it going? the text comes in at 4:45 pm from Adele. "Great," I type. "Better than great."

"Is he behaving?"

"Deke or Scott?" I type, feeling cheeky.

BOTH, she texts back.

"Scott's himself. Deke's perfect." Too perfect. Today was unreal. The helicopter ride, the picnic date… but after Teddy dropped us back off at the resort, Deke excused himself, and I haven't seen him since. "Got shit to do." I'm disappointed—after our date I was hoping for some alone time with him. Getting to know him, horizontally. In *bed.*

So much for Operation Seduce Sadie.

He's a perfect gentleman, I clarify to Adele.

He better be.

I smile and tuck my phone away in my clutch. Tonight is the rehearsal dinner, and I've spent the last hour getting dolled up.

Deke appears right as I'm doing a final lipstick check. He takes the bathroom and emerges dressed in very credible rehearsal dinner wear—a dark blazer over his usual black jeans and a black T. It works, even with his beat up motorcycle boots.

"Hey," I smile at him. "Ready to do this?"

He nods and bends down to kiss my cheek. But he's sober, shut down. Remote behind his aviator shades.

"What is it?" I ask. "What's wrong?"

He shakes his head, and with a hand on my back, escorts me out of our room and down to the lobby to meet up with the bridal party. I put on my game face and air kiss all the bridesmaids. Deke remains at my side, a tall, silent shadow. Eventually we head out to run through the ceremony. There's an air of excitement, and when Jenn, the bride to be, arrives, we all squeal and clap.

"This is it," I remind myself. "This is why we're here." For my friend's big day.

Everything goes smoothly, but I can't help turning my head to check on Deke every few minutes. He sits in the audience on the bride's side, staring off into the distance. Playing the part of bored boyfriend, except he's not bored. This is Broody Deke. His mood reminds me of how he acted after our kiss in the alley way, when the clam-jamming biker came by.

He stirs a little when Scott escorts me down the aisle, but Scott behaves himself. I'll bet he senses the unspoken threat from Deke if he doesn't.

When I take my place, I search Deke out. I can't see his eyes because he's still wearing his badass aviator shades, even though the sun's almost down behind the mountains. I make a note to tease him about wearing his sunglasses at night and give him a smile. Deke lifts his chin in response.

I'm going to figure out what put him in this broody mood. Seductive Sadie is making her debut tonight.

Rehearsal ends, and we all head off to dinner. A few people mention the helicopter, and Deke finds himself briefly the center of attention. I'm able and willing to step in to deflect questions, but Deke handles it. "Teddy's Helicopter Tours," he says, handing out business cards. "Check 'em out."

"Quite the impression your man is making," Elana purrs in my ear as I stand by watching Deke talk to the curious crowd about helicopter tours. He is patient and calm, even leaning down to converse with Jenn's grandma, who's in a wheelchair. She pats his cheek, smiling up at him.

"He's a good man," Elana tells me, her eyes glued to Deke's ass as he's bent over. When he rises, he's a full head taller than everyone.

"Mmm," I murmur into my champagne.

Elana stops ogling Deke and faces me fully. "Way better than your ex. What did you even see in him?"

"I don't even know. Thanks. I thought it'd be awkward with you here."

"On no, hun, I'm just here to make him look good. He made it worth my while, if you know what I mean." Her eyes twinkle over her vodka tonic. "But I'd never hurt a sister. We've got to stick together."

I clink glasses with her. She looks around swiftly and leans in close to whisper a warning, "Scott wanted to try to ambush you at the hot tub. But the rate he's going, he'll pass out tonight. At least, I hope." Elana wrinkles her nose. "Does he always snore?"

"Yeah. Sorry."

"It's fine, I've got earplugs."

Deke turns, looking over the crowd at me.

"Go, get your man," Elana waves me away.

I cut through the crowd and thread my arm through Deke's. "Come on, honey," I say loudly for everyone to hear. "There's something I need to show you."

Deke

SADIE GRABS my hand and tugs me out of the crowd. I follow willingly, feeling relief as she leads me out of the room.

"Everything okay?" I ask as she pulls me into a side hall. She glances around and pushes me into an alcove before gazing up at me.

"You looked like you needed a break."

The tension in my spine ebbs away. She's right. For a moment, I was close to losing it. Too many people around. My wolf was agitated, but just being near Sadie helps.

I let my head drop and press my forehead against hers, breathing her in. She's my calm in the storm.

Leaving her is gonna suck. My wolf is already frantic, imagining it.

"I want to thank you," she whispers.

"Sadie." I don't mean to touch her—not after my conversation with Rafe, but I find myself rubbing my thumb along her lower lip. My cock wants in that lush mouth again.

But I can't. This is so fucked up.

I drop my hand and rub the back of my neck. Rafe's last words ring in my head. *You're a danger to her. Get out as soon as you can, before it's too late.*

He's right. I'm a monster. *I destroy everything I touch.*

My wolf howls in my chest. I groan, pressing a hand to my chest. I feel like I'm having a fucking heart attack. But I'm not. It's my wolf, grieving like it's lost its mate.

Could Sadie actually be my mate?

I'm an idiot for not realizing it sooner. I've had the urge to mark her every time we get sexual, but I chalked it up to my wolf being nuts.

Wolves don't usually pick humans for mates, but I do know it happens. Especially with our species' dwindling numbers, I hear of it more and more often these days.

Sadie's touch brings me back to her. "What is happening? What's wrong?"

Even just the thought of her being my mate brings my wolf roaring to the surface, my teeth itching to descend and mark her. "I shouldn't be here," I mutter.

"No," she says. "Don't say that. You're here to help me. You're doing great. I'm sorry I had to drag you into this."

"Babe." I let my head drop to her shoulder, into the curve of her neck and breathe in her scent. It helps. My wolf calms. "It's not that. I'm glad to be here. I'd fight to be by your side."

She inhales quickly and brings her small hand to cup my neck, holding me against her. "You don't have to fight. I'm right here."

Fuck. I can't fight this any longer. I lift my head, cup her cheeks and kiss her, hard.

A loud group of party-goers passes the hall, and I tuck her deeper in the alcove.

They're right around the corner, anyone could walk down the hall and see us, but Sadie doesn't seem to care.

"I want you," she breathes. "I need you."

And who am I to deny her anything?

Sadie

Deke's big hands grip my head, holding me still for his kiss. He backs me against the wall and presses himself against me. And I feel him—all of him. Either there's a giant gun in his pants, or he's excited to see me.

My pussy spasms. "Yes," I breathe.

He kisses down my neck, his right hand still gripping my hair. He tugs me into position, taking control. His other hand finds the edge of my cute little dress and starts to draw it upwards.

And then I realize I've made a mistake.

"Wait," I gasp although I hate to slow him down.

"Not waiting," Deke growls. "You want this."

"No, not that, I do want you, but this dress...it's pretty tight and…" I trail off, wishing I didn't have to explain. "I'm wearing...shapewear."

His brows knit together, and he slips his hands under my dress, where he

encounters what I've been trying to tell him about.

"What is this?" he growls, sliding his hand along the tight bodysuit, trying to find my skin. "It's like armor."

"Yep. Girl armor. Guys wear it too. I think Scott has some although he'd never admit it."

"Fuck." His hand goes between my legs, where the bodysuit has made me smooth and sexless as a Barbie doll. "It's a fucking chastity belt."

I let out a hysterical giggle. "Yes."

His laugh is pained.

"Fudge." I press my center against his palm, grinding. "Just tear it." I feel his nails scrabbling along the sausage-casing-like tube, trying to find purchase, so he can rip the damn thing off me. Meanwhile, I'm about to explode from the friction of his demanding touch.

"Fuck this shit," he snarls and grabs my hips. He lifts me bodily, so I'm hitched up between the wall and him, straddling his leg above the knee.

"Grind down, baby," he orders, and I do. I grab his shoulders and ride his thick thigh, dragging my greedy pussy up and down. The prominent ridge of his quads provides the perfect place for me to rub. I rock my hips, angling so the hard muscle rubs me just right.

There's a rip, and Deke drags the top of my dress down. His fingers find the top of my strapless bra and tug it down. He bows his head and licks my nipple.

"Oh fudge." I brace my hands on his broad shoulders, dig my nails into the bunched muscles like granite under my palms, and rock my hips faster. Deke groans, pressing me up against the wall.

"I'm close."

"Thank fuck." He hitches me up higher, and a little growl escapes my throat. I surge against him, trying to find the right amount of friction.

"That's it, baby. Take it."

My orgasm rises, white hot, burning my brain. I press my face into Deke's shoulder, and as I climax, I bite down to stop my cry.

"Fuck," he grunts.

"Oh God," I pant. "Oh God." There are voices outside the hall. I want to scream at them to go away. "We have to get back to the party."

"Fuck that." He bundles me in his coat to cover my torn dress and scoops me into his arms. "Our room. Our bed. Now."

Sadie

To my delight, Deke uses his stealth superpowers to slip past the party undetected and carry me to our room.

Once there, he sets me down and turns to lock the door.

I back into the dark room, letting his jacket fall from my shoulders. My torn dress gapes open at the front. I raise my hands to fix it, and Deke growls.

"Your eyes," I murmur as he prowls forward, and I back away slowly. His eyes seem to glint in the dark like a cat's—a bright green. Shivers run up my spine at the sight of him, a predator looming in the darkness, stalking me.

"Take off your clothes," he growls.

I halt, and I raise my chin, standing my ground, delighting in this game.

"Or what?" I challenge playfully.

"Or I'll remove them for you."

"Promise?" My voice is breathy. Breath*less*.

He moves faster than a guy his size should be capable of. His hands are on me, ripping fabric. With a few harsh cracks of sound, my dress and shapewear are no more. I can't say that I regret it.

I kick the remains of the fabric away. I'm naked but for a bra and a tiny lace scrap of panties.

"Your turn," I say and put eager hands on him.

His t-shirt feels as soft as it looks. I whip the dark fabric off, revealing the toned, tanned expanse of Deke's chest.

"I need you," I gasp. "Now." My hands fumble at the button of his jeans. Things aren't happening fast enough.

"I'll give you what you need," he murmurs.

I give a fake growl and shove him down onto the bed. He lets me push him, falling backwards, his gaze undressing me as I climb over him. I am Naughty Sadie. Sadie Uncaged.

"Eager, baby?" he asks, chuckling.

"Shut up." I grin, and I straddle him and work open the button on his pants. My thighs strain as they splay over his giant frame.

His big hands cup my butt. "You're a bad girl."

"Yes. Yes, I am."

His eyes light with green-gold flame. He rolls, so I'm under him then flips me over and smacks my ass. "Bad, bad girl."

"Yes." I knead the bedspread with my hands, bracing myself and pushing my ass up in the air. "Yes, I am."

Deke smacks my ass again. "Bad girl." He drapes his lower half over me, rubbing his cock into the crack of my ass. Then he lifts off and spanks me harder.

I hiss, gritting my teeth against the sting of his palm. Deep inside, the pain undergoes some beautiful alchemy, so with each smack, bliss radiates from my core. I moan and push back into his punishing hand.

"Fuck, yes," he mutters. And then my panties are off, and his mouth is on my backside, his stubbles scraping the chastised skin.

I cry out as he licks between my cheeks, a delicious sensation that's oh-so-taboo. I tilt my hips inviting him to lick me lower down. His tongue flicks my entrance.

"Fudge!" I pant, crying out for more.

He rolls me back over. I love how strong and sure he is. How easily he takes charge and positions me. I don't have to worry or wonder if I'm doing something right. He makes it all so easy.

He tugs the cups of my bra down and palms my breasts, squeezing, then brushing his thumbs across my tightened nipples. When he lowers his mouth to take one between his lips, I arch up, moaning. He sucks my nipple, nips it lightly while he kneads my other breast.

Feeling bold—because Deke always makes me feel bold—I push his head lower.

When he lifts his head, his grin is feral. He moves lower.

Deke pushes my knees wide and licks into me, his tongue parting my nether lips, tracing around the insides.

Shiver after shiver of pleasure ripple through me. "Yes," I moan.

He penetrates me with his tongue then swirls it around my clit.

"Please," I pant.

He circles it again, then flicks it with the tip of his tongue over and over again. I lift my hips, chasing the sensation. My entire body is a live wire, radiating with unspent energy.

Deke slides a finger inside me. It feels delicious, especially when he strokes my inner wall. But I want more. "Deke," I gasp. "I want you."

His head jerks up, and he stares at me with those green-lit

eyes. His expression is almost alarmed, and for a moment I fear I've come on too strong. That he's going to back off again. But then he gets up and shucks his jeans and briefs, retrieving a condom from his wallet.

I unfasten my bra and untangle myself from it, squirming around on the bed, fully naked. Ready.

So ready.

I've never been so enthusiastic for sex in my life. Deke makes everything thrilling. Anything possible.

He pounces over me with a lightness that seems at odds with his large size and nuzzles into my neck, kissing and biting.

I arch to rub my breasts over his hard chest, my head falling back. I cling to his huge arms, trying to pull his body down over mine. "I need you," I repeat, still half-afraid he's going to back off.

"I'm gonna give it to you," he promises, ripping the condom wrapper with his teeth and then rolling it on. He drags the sheathed head of his cock through my wetness. I plant my feet wide, knees wide apart to receive him. I tip my hips up.

His face contorts as if in pain as he eases into me. "Sadie," he rasps. "Fuck."

"Yes!" Oh, heck yes. I thrust up to take him deeper because he's going too slow, and he curses again.

"Deke, yes." I grab his muscled butt and pull him all the way in, wrapping my legs around his back and hooking my ankles.

A shudder of pleasure runs through him, and he starts undulating slowly. It's like beautiful, art-film porn. Our bodies are locked together, and we move as one—him giving, me receiving. I don't know how long the perfect, mindless pleasure goes on, but soon it's not enough. I bite his shoulder.

Unlock my ankles and bring my knees up toward my shoulders, spreading myself wide.

More pain flickers over Deke's face. "Fuck, Sadie." He holds my knees and pumps faster, his loins slapping against mine in a delicious rhythm. I stroke my hands everywhere they'll reach, loving the feel of his skin, the tone of his huge muscles.

"Yes," I encourage. It feels incredible. "Deke."

"Sadie," he rasps, rising to his knees and lifting my hips into the air, his large hands gripping my butt as he pumps into me.

"Oh my God," I pant, nearly out of my mind. I've never had sex like this—so uninhibited and raw. So beautiful and natural and easy.

He gives his head a shake, like he's trying to clear it. For a moment, I see the glint of his teeth, and they almost appear sharper. Longer. But it must be the way they glow in the moonlight streaming through the window.

He shakes his head again and pulls out, flipping me back over and arranging me on my knees. When he enters me from behind, it's pure heaven. He gets in deep. I instinctively drop to my elbow to roll my hips even higher, to make the angle even better.

Deke grips my hips and slams in, seeming to lose control. His breath rasps, ragged and harsh. His loins slap against my butt, filling the room with the delicious sounds of our love-making.

"Sadie." His shout is a warning.

"Yes, please," I cry. I'm so ready to come, I'm just waiting for him.

"Sadie," he chokes again. I absolutely adore hearing my name in that strained, guttural tone. Like he can't hold back.

Like I drive him wild. It's so different from the quick, boring interludes Scott and I used to have.

"Give it to me, Deke," I rasp.

His shout almost sounds like a roar. Or an animalistic snarl. He buries deep inside me, his fingers squeezing my hips with a bruising grip.

"Yes!" I cry, my muscles spasming around his cock, my own orgasm cresting and splashing over me. "Yes, Deke, oh God."

He bumps my butt in several tiny thrusts, wringing out more pleasure from me. More squeezing of my internal muscles. More ripples of pleasure.

I love you. The words are in my head, but fortunately, I stop myself from saying them. I don't know what this means to Deke. I mean, I know he didn't fake it.

There was nothing fake about anything we just did.

But it might have just been sex.

Which is fine.

Totally fine.

Oh God, it's not fine. I don't know why I thought I'd be happy with just having Deke for the weekend.

Now I want him for keeps, and he's already made it clear he can't be that for me.

Deke

OH FUCK, I nearly marked her. My teeth descended during sex, coated with the serum that would permanently embed my scent in her skin. I almost marked and claimed Sadie as my mate, which would permanently bind her to me.

I was able to hold back, though, and still give Sadie what she needed.

A surge of satisfaction runs through me at that. I did have the discipline to keep my wolf in check. For Sadie, I did it.

For Sadie, I could do anything.

I ease out and dispose of the condom. My wolf is agitated, pissed that I didn't mark her, but I have him under control. As soon as she's asleep, I'll get outside and run it off.

For now, though, I can't bring myself to leave her side. Not when she's leaning up on her elbow, looking so fucking vulnerable. I come back to the bed and pull the covers down, helping her into them before I slide in beside her.

She immediately rolls her sweet, soft body into mine, resting her head on the place where shoulder meets arm, stroking her fingernails through the curls of my chest hair. "Thank you," she murmurs.

Even though I just came, my dick punches out at the honey-sweet sound. The suggestion that I satisfied her, getting me revved up to do it again.

A dozen different answers flip through my head. Glib ones like, "At your service" or boastful like, "there's more where that came from." But none of them do her justice. None of them fit the beauty of the sex we just had—and I swear to fate, I've never called sex beautiful before in my life.

But with Sadie it was. Even the part where my wolf fought for control and wanted to mark her. It all felt right. Protecting her from my wolf felt right, and wanting to mark her also felt right.

I settle for a rumble of assent and kiss her head.

In a few moments, her breath lengthens, and she falls asleep. I wait another half an hour, savoring the feel of her in my arms, before I slip out of bed to shift and run.

CHAPTER 12

eke

As soon as Sadie stirs in the morning, I return to the bed. I hadn't trusted myself after the run to sleep beside her, so I dozed in the chair by the door. It felt right to guard her, keep her safe.

"Deke." She yawns, curling into me. I grit my teeth as she brushes against my cock, and it hardens to steel.

"Morning, baby." I dip my head and kiss her, my tongue teasing out her secret longing, stroking the silken cave of her mouth. She moans and arches against me. I scent her wet heat.

I pull away and clear my throat. "It's almost nine."

"Is it? Fudge." She sits up.

"Fudge," I repeat because it's so damn cute. "Do you ever curse?"

"Yes." She grins. "But not often. I would hate to inadvertently do it in front of my kids."

She pecks my lips again. "I've got to go. We have a spa day all day, and I'll be getting ready with the bride." She bites her lip, and I want to mark her so bad, my canines ache. "You're invited to lunch with the groom and the groomsmen. It'll be a bunch of dudebros in tuxes, and Scott will be there. You could keep an eye on him. I know it sucks—"

"I'll pass," I say immediately. "Don't worry, I'll entertain myself." I cup her cheek.

She grabs my wrist and slides one of my fingers into her mouth. Her lips surround it, and she sucks, hard.

"Just a promise of what's to come," she says and scampers off the bed quickly but not quickly enough. I snake a hand out and smack her ass, hard. She jumps but smiles, and I almost chase her down. She'll have the memory of my handprint on her through the morning.

~

Sadie

The day of the wedding passes in a blur. Spa morning then getting the bride ready. The whole time I want to be with Deke instead. Back up on the mountain having a picnic. Or taking a hike. Or… having another round between the sheets.

But I do my part supporting the bride. Getting into my grape purple bridesmaid dress. Jenn is a lovely bride in a short and sculptural wedding dress. It's beautiful and modern, with a collar that flares up at the top in an asymmetrical line, making her look like a white calla lily.

As planned, Scott walks me down the aisle.

"You look beautiful," he whispers, a minute before we start.

"I know," I say. "Deke told me." I actually haven't seen Deke yet, but I look for his dark head and broad shoulders, rising taller than anyone else in the seats. And when I find him, he's looking straight back at me. I smile and wave and am rewarded with a subtle nod. Not an overflow of emotion but plenty encouraging in Deke-speak. *You got this, baby.*

As I walk down the aisle, I hold Deke's gaze as long as I can. I hardly notice Scott's frustration, even though it radiates from him. I started out needing Deke as a shield from Scott's pressure, but now it just bounces off me. I could care less what the man beside me wants. I'm way more interested in what I want, and that's Deke.

As Jenn and Geoff say their vows, I seek out Deke again. He said he'd never get married. I wonder why. We've grown closer this weekend, but not so close that his secrets aren't a chasm between us. A chasm I intend to cross.

"Great job, baby," Deke tells me after the ceremony. He tugs at the flimsy strap holding up my bodice. "You wearing shapewear under this?"

Laughter rockets out of me, and I cover my mouth to stifle it. "Nope," I whisper back. "I learned my lesson." He moves closer, his lips finding my ear, and I duck my head. "Not yet," I warn. "I have to do pictures with the bridal party. Then the reception."

"Fuck the reception," Deke murmurs, and my pussy clenches.

"I would love to screw instead of going to the reception," I murmur, watching his eyes heat, "but we have to stay until they cut the cake. And a few dances."

"Okay." He removes his hand and smoothes the front of his tux. In his bowtie and cumberbund, he looks like a sexier and more dangerous James Bond. "But it'll cost ya."

"I can't wait until you collect," I murmur back and obey

Brigit's summons to do pictures with the bride and groom. I can't help glancing over at him the whole time, and he seems to always be watching me. His eyes flash oddly in the low light.

Later, after the meal and the speeches, Deke and I dance cheek to cheek to Frank Sinatra. Well, not cheek to cheek—he's too tall. But I lay my head on his chest, and it's perfect.

"Thank you for coming with me this weekend." I lift my head to meet his warm gaze.

His eyes crinkle, but he doesn't quite smile. His smiles are rare, which makes it all the more exciting when I win one.

"I know this isn't your scene at all. This was a huge favor to ask…" I guess I'm fishing. I feel like last night proved we've gone way beyond the fake date thing, but I'm honestly still not sure where we stand. The fact that he doesn't want to marry and have kids should've made me stop hoping for something more, but it hasn't. I've already fallen for this guy.

I want it all.

We dance past the gift table, piled high with everything a couple could want to start married life, including an entire set of Le Creuset cookware.

"Sadie." Deke looks uncomfortable.

Oh God, he's going to let me down gently now.

"I can't be in a relationship. I'm… dangerous."

I blink up at him. Finally, we're getting things into the open. "Is this about the, um assault charges?"

"Yeah."

"What happened?" My heart's pounding, but I want to know everything, whatever it is.

"I get… protective. Over-protective. I was at a bar, and a woman seemed like she was getting hassled. I stepped in. But I sort of lost control. My wo—" He stops and gives his head a quick shake. "I used excessive force. I didn't mean to, but I hurt the guys more than was necessary."

"You don't know your own strength," I murmur.

"No," he cuts me off sharply. "I do. Which is why that never should've happened. I should've kept control. Especially with civilians."

I swallow. "It's part of the PTSD, Deke. You've had to kill in the line of duty, right?"

He draws in a sharp breath then lets it out slowly. "Yeah. I… sometimes still do." His gaze locks on my face, like he's watching for signs that I'm horrified.

I am a little, but I'm careful to school my features. I should have guessed at this when he mentioned the multi-million dollar government contracts. No wonder they're not allowed to date. They're like… government hitmen. Or something.

I try on that idea to see if it makes me want to run screaming from Deke.

It doesn't.

I lift my chin. "I don't care," I tell him.

He cocks his head. "You… you don't? I mean, you should. Sadie, I'm not safe."

I stop dancing and reach up, holding his face in both my hands. "You're safe for me," I tell him.

He hesitates. "I don't know, Sadie. Those guys at the bar…"

"You went into attack mode because you thought you had to. It was a mistake. Deke, no one's perfect."

"I want to be for you."

My heart lurches. He said *for you.*

He wants to be perfect for me.

Deke wants to be mine!

"Perfect is overrated. Perfect is what Scott and my dad

want. They don't care about the inside, so long as the outside looks good."

Deke looks uncertain.

"You're a good man, Deke. You protect those who can't protect themselves. You have honor. Commitment. I don't want you perfect. I just want you."

Deke draws another quick breath, his eyes flashing green. His mouth descends on mine. Crashes down on my lips. Claims them. His large palm cups the back of my head, and his tongue sweeps between my lips.

I hear some giggles and murmurs around us. We're standing in the middle of the dance floor, making out like wild, unruly teenagers.

It feels wonderful.

The kiss goes on forever. Long enough that I'm sure Deke's forgotten where we are, so I pull away, laughing. "Let's go upstairs," I say.

He doesn't hesitate. He sweeps me up in his arms, like I'm the bride, and carries me out of the ballroom.

Once we're in the dark hotel room, it feels like everything moves in slow motion. He puts me down and silently unzips me. In the big bay window, the full moon shines her silvery light, gilding the dark earth with a magical aura. Fresh arousal blooms inside me, my pulse a steady drumbeat.

I let the gown pool at my feet and turn to face Deke in nothing but a thong. He's stepped back, standing in the shadows. In his tux, he's so handsome, I could cry.

He looks like he's holding back again.

I take a step towards him. "I want you. *You*, Deke." His scent flows over me, making me giddy, spinning me out. I don't know if it's pheromones or the full moon. I'm going wild.

"Sadie, there's more—" he says, but I grab him, mashing my mouth against his.

"I don't care," I mutter. "Whatever it is, I want you, anyway."

He growls against my lips and rears up, ripping off his shirt, revealing his stunning torso. *Oh yes.* My ovaries are twerking. *Let's take this sex train to O town!*

~

Deke

"SADIE-GIRL. I'm gonna fuck you so hard."

Whoa. I don't know where that came from. It definitely fell on the wrong side of the respect line, but Sadie doesn't seem to mind. Her nimble fingers work the button on my tuxedo pants.

This woman is a gift. A fucking gift.

I stroke my hands up the bare skin of her back, mating our mouths again. I wanted to tell her about my wolf—bare all my secrets to her—but when she gave me an excuse not to, I took it.

Telling her is forbidden. I know what Rafe would say. What he'd say about all of this.

But I can't hold back where Sadie's concerned. Everything about her feels right. Her scent. The way her presence both calms and incites my wolf, her sweet, sweet acceptance of my dark side.

I love her.

I'm not sure I even knew what love is until this moment.

Wolves don't think in those terms. We mate by scent, by fate, not by human emotion. But what I feel for Sadie is real.

It's beyond scent and the drive to mark her. It's about who she is. How she makes me feel. The man I want to be for her.

I want to keep Sadie Diaz. Mate her. Marry her. Everything.

The moment she gets my pants down my hips, I step out of them and walk her backwards to the bed. Her knees hit the mattress, and she falls backward, my hand behind her head to gentle the landing.

I crawl over her, then remember a condom. I quickly kick off my briefs, retrieve a rubber and come back to the bed.

Sadie's wearing a tiny thong. Her skin glows bronze in the moonlight. I bite the string of the panties and drag them down her legs with my teeth. Her laughter is musical and sweet. I kiss my way up her leg, starting with the calf, moving to the inner thigh and up to the apex. I lay a soft kiss on her mound, then push her legs open.

"Spread for me, baby," I tell her.

She moans softly before my tongue even touches her. I lick into her, parting her lips and dragging my tongue through her wetness. I swirl around her entrance then around her clit.

"You're so good at that." She sounds breathless. Already desperate. I want to keep her that way all night long.

"I'm gonna make you come so hard," I boast, sliding a finger inside her.

She squirms to take it deeper, and I back it out and slip in two digits, using them to caress her inner wall. I find her G-spot, feel the tissue tighten beneath the pads of my fingertips.

Her legs thrash around me, and she cries out. I lave her clit, suck the tiny nubbin as I continue to rub her G-spot.

"Deke! Oh God, it's so good."

I hum against her flesh. Or maybe it's a growl. It doesn't matter. I'm in control. She's given me strength with her trust.

I'm not going to mark her. I'm going to make her come like she's never come before.

I pump my fingers, bumping into her G-spot with each thrust. She screams and tears at my hair, pressing my face into her flesh, even though I never stopped sucking that sweet little clit.

Her hips jerk and convulse. Her channel squeezes and pumps my fingers as she comes. I stop pumping while she goes off, then slow my stroking, bringing on a second release. I release my suction-hold on her clit and flick it with my tongue. A third after-shock rolls through her.

"Oh my God," she pants. "Deke. It's so good." She tugs my ears to lift my head from her swollen flesh. "Come here," she begs. "I need you inside me."

I grin, her juices coating my lips. "I am inside you." I stroke her G-spot again to remind her, and a fourth tidal wave hits.

"What about.... Um... fucking me so hard?"

A chuckle rumbles out of me. "Sadie Diaz, did you just say *fuck* instead of *fudge*?"

She laughs. "It seemed appropriate."

"Mmm." I crawl up over her. She's right. It does seem appropriate. I pick up the condom package, which I'd dropped on the bed, and rip it open. "I *did* promise you a good fucking, didn't I?"

"Uh huh." Her knees drop open, and her eyelids droop in anticipation. She may be sweet, but she's not prude. She's *adorable*.

I roll the condom on and rise up on my knees, lining the head of my cock up with her entrance. "Making you come is a fucking priviledge, Sadie Diaz."

Shit, I have zero filters tonight. The relief of having my

darkness exposed to her and her acceptance of it utterly changed me.

A shiver ripples through her, and her kiss-swollen lips part. She reaches for my cock and fists it firmly, guiding me in. “I need you,” she repeats.

Fuck. I need her, too.

So badly.

One stroke inside her, and I’m lost. The moon already has my blood hot. My canines lengthen, but I close my mouth firmly around them. I’m going to keep control. For Sadie, I can do it.

I slam into her with more force than I intend, but she arches and moans with satisfaction, as if it was exactly the thing she needed. “I’m gonna fuck you until you can’t walk straight tomorrow.”

I ease back and slam home again, firm and sure. Her head slides up the bed, and I have to catch her shoulder to keep it from hitting the headboard.

“F-fuck me, Deke.”

I don’t know why hearing her say the word *fuck* undoes me. Because it’s so unlike her. Because it means she really wants this.

I snap my hips faster, plunging in and out, watching her face for signs I’m being too rough.

I don’t see any, though. She seems to want every bit I want to give. She’s gorgeous—her thick, dark hair spread out on the pillow in a halo around her head. Her beautiful breasts pointing toward the ceiling, nipples tight and eager for my mouth. I bend and take one between my lips, sucking it.

She moans her pleasure.

The sound makes me snap my hips hard again, the pressure building at the base of my spine.

“Yes,” she encourages.

I suck the other nipple, so it doesn't feel left out.

She pinches one of mine, which makes me smile.

"You want it hard?" I ask, belatedly, because I'm already fucking her hard. Maybe I just need to be sure.

"Yes!" she agrees. "I want it so hard."

"Oh fuck." I brace my hand against the headboard and work my cock between her legs—fast, with short thrusts—*in, in, in, in*. Each time I do, she lets out a high-pitched "*uhn, uhn, uhn, uhn*" that drives me fucking wild.

I'm sure the entire resort floor can hear us going at it, and that makes my wolf proud as hell.

I brace with both hands and arc into her, even faster. Even harder.

Her wild gaze is on my face. Her lips stay open for her cries of pleasure. The bed rocks against the wall, slamming into it again and again.

My wolf snarls, wanting me to set him free, dying to mark her. But I resist.

For Sadie, I resist.

"Oh Deke. Please… *please*!" she's begging me. To stop? To come?

Just the thought of coming makes it happen. I wanted to fuck her all night, but the pleasure was too intense. Cum shoots down my staff. Sadie wraps her legs around me and pulls me deeper, holding me in as we both reach orgasm in perfect concert.

I let out a strangled shout. My wolf hurtles my head down into the crook of her neck, teeth ready to sink into her flesh, but at the last moment, I throw it back, like a man howling at the moon. A man-wolf, telling the whole fucking world he's found his female.

His mate.

Mark her, my wolf whimpers.

Not yet.

He seems to sense the promise in my warning. That I *do* plan to mark her, just not tonight. My canines retract again.

Sadie's safe.

Sadie's mine.

As for telling her I'm a wolf, as for marking her—we'll get there. When I'm certain I can always keep her safe.

Safe from my wolf and my darkness.

CHAPTER 13

adie

I WAKE IN A WARM BED. Alone, but there's a note on the pillow from Deke.

Gone for a run.

I smile and stretch, feeling good from my hair-sprayed head to my pointed toes. Mission *Seduce Deke* went well.

We're leaving today. Our fake boyfriend operation will be over. No promises on how our relationship will continue, but after the talk we had last night, I have so much optimism that we can work things out.

I pull on my hiking boots and head outside. The resort is quiet this morning, with barely anyone about. The rest of the wedding party will be sleeping late.

Outside the air is fresh and clean. It's the perfect morning for a hike. Hopefully, I'll run into Deke, and we can pick up where we left off.

I bounce down the hiking trail, quickly leaving the green

resort grounds for a worn, rocky path. A twig snaps behind me.

"Deke?" I call, turning and heading back the way I came.

"Sadie." Scott steps out from behind a bushy bristlecone pine tree.

Ew! Total creeper! I skid to a halt. "Scott."

"We need to talk." His voice is hoarse. He's still in his tux from last night. His eyes are red and his breath stinks like vodka.

Yuck.

"Did you even sleep last night?"

"Can't sleep." He seizes my arms, and I get a whiff of his foul breath mixed with stale cologne up close. I gag, trying to push him off.

"Go away." I manage to get free. He trips on a rock, trying to follow.

"Sadie, I want to be with you."

"No. You just think someone's playing with your toy. I never meant anything to you. It was about my dad's contacts. You can't get development projects through the town council without his support."

"Fuck, Sadie, no." He staggers forward and falls on me, his heavy weight dragging me down. I scream and try to wrench my jacket out of his grip.

"Scott, you're hurting me—"

A savage growl sounds from the slope above us. Every hair on my body bristles in warning.

Predator!

My muscles turn to stone, and I stop fighting Scott, who fumbles, pawing at me, before standing straight, belatedly turning towards the threat. There's another growl, and a huge black shape bounds down the slope toward us.

"Wha—?" Scott's question is cut off by the giant shadow slamming into him. He goes down flailing, and I scream.

Scott lands on the ground, and over him stands the biggest, baddest black wolf I've ever seen.

I stumble backward. My boot hits a rock, and I fall, catching myself at the last moment. The wolf's head turns toward me, and I flinch.

Then it swivels back to Scott, opens its giant jaws and lets out a growl that's more like a roar.

Run! Adrenaline screams in my veins.

Scott lets out a high-pitched squeal. Fudge, he's about to get eaten. I have to do something! My legs wobble.

"No!" I snap in my sternest teacher voice. Without thinking, I grab a branch to beat the wolf off of him.

Before I can swing, the wolf backs off. Somehow Scott scrambles upwards.

"Hey!" I try to distract the wolf, so Scott can get away—and he does, hightailing it up to the resort, his shredded tux tails flapping in his wake. Leaving me with the wolf.

Alone.

What a prick.

I take a backward step and adjust my grip on the branch. *Fudge.*

"This is not how I thought I'd go," I tell the wolf.

To my utter shock, the wolf sits and whines.

Like a freaking pet!

"Um… okay. Good wolf." I take a slow step backward.

He watches me. There's no sign of his teeth, but I'll never forget the sight of them. This beast is a killer. And I can't outrun him—I saw how fast he came down that mountainside.

What am I going to do?

He starts toward me—not in a lunge. More of a trot, but I

flinch. The moment I do, he stops and sits again. Then I catch a glint of silver in the thick ruff around its neck. The wolf turns its head, and the flat silver rectangle catches the light more clearly.

I gasp. "Th-those are Deke's! You're wearing Deke's dog tags." What does this mean? Goose flesh crawls up my arms.

I put my hand over my mouth. There are two options here. The wolf either ate Deke and is wearing his dog tags as a trophy or…

"Sherlock Holmes said, *Once you eliminate the impossible, whatever remains must be the truth,"* I say in a shaky voice.

The wolf cocks its head to the side, like it's listening.

"You either ate Deke, or… you *are* Deke."

The wolf chuffs and jerks its head like it's nodding.

But no. That's impossible. "You better not have eaten Deke," I laugh-cry, semi-hysterical. "He's my boyfriend, and I really like him." I lift the branch, fully prepared to avenge my lover.

The wolf drops to its belly and crawls forward in supplication.

"D-deke?" It's so ridiculous, so impossible, and yet… those green eyes. I've definitely seen them before. Now I understand why they glowed in the dark.

The wolf gets up and trots behind some bushes. A low growling sound makes tingles rise on my skin, and then Deke, my giant, muscled boyfriend rises from the wolf's hiding place.

I stagger backwards because my legs are confused. *Fight or flight? Run or hug Deke?*

I settle for licking my lips. "You're a wolf," I state the obvious. The impossible.

Deke hesitates, like he's not sure if he should approach.

"Don't be afraid," he murmurs, hands open. Deke prowls out from the brush. Without the bushes between us, I realize something else.

My lips twitch. "Um, you're naked." Except for the dog tags. Those glint on his impressive chest, drawing the eye to the cut rows of his abs, then down, following his happy trail to…

Okay. So evidence suggests he and the wolf did not switch places. That they are, in fact, one and the same.

"You're a…" I can't say it. It's too insane.

He nods. "That's my darkest secret."

I drag my eyes back up to his face. It's hard. There's so much of him for my eyes to feast on. "Okay."

His brows shoot up. "Okay? Is that all you're going to say?"

"What should I say? Did you expect me to run screaming?"

He shrugs. "Pretty much."

"Well I'm not. I'm not sure I can run, actually. Excuse me." I drop down onto a large rock because my legs stop working.

Deke squats slowly, tucking his entire body into a crouch, so our eyes are still level. His movements are eerily fluid. Like the wolf's.

"You're a wolf," I repeat.

He nods.

I reach out and touch his wolf tattoo. "Oh my God." I pass a shaking hand over my face. I have this insane urge to laugh. "Oh my God. This is your secret."

He's motionless, waiting. Waiting for me to pass judgement or tell him to leave or something. Just waiting.

"You're a wolf," I say wonderingly and touch his face. He

closes his eyes and turns his head, so I'm stroking back his hair. Petting him. "Deke," I whisper.

"Sadie," he groans into my palm. He nips at my skin.

And then I wrap my arms around him and kiss him. He kisses me back. I surge over him, bearing him down to his shins, so I can straddle his waist. "Is this okay? Am I hurting you?"

"No," he says between rough kisses. "It doesn't hurt anymore."

Before I can ask what he means, he's got his hand down the back of my leggings. I groan as he cups me from behind, his fingers seeking my heat.

It's the work of a second for me to kick off my boots and wriggle and tug them off. He's already naked, all six feet plus of him.

"I don't have a condom, Sadie-girl." He looks pained.

"Oh." Nope, I do not accept clam-jam this time. "You could pull out?"

"Deal." His biceps bulge as he picks me up by the waist and lowers me over his dick. He's unbelievably strong. Now I know why it was so simple for him to just pick me up and carry me off whenever he had the urge.

Deke lifts and lowers me over his cock, slowly at first, then working up to a bounce. My breasts rise and fall with the momentum, and I feel porn-star sexy. It's delicious. I'm screwing a werewolf. Under the open sky.

It's perfect.

His stubble scrapes my face as we kiss. I cry out as all the danger and adrenaline and threat roll into some primal feeling, an epic orgasm to celebrate the way I faced the wolf and survived. I'm alive.

Deke groans his eyes changing to green. "I can't," he mutters. I catch the glint of wolf-teeth in his mouth. "I can't."

Can't what? I want to ask but he's still bouncing me, pushing me towards another climax. This time, when I break, he curses, lifts me off him, and pumps his cock to release onto the soft earth. His breath blows harsh against my jacket, and as he comes, he slashes his lip with a sharp tooth, sending blood dripping down his chin.

~

Deke

"FUCK, I'M SORRY," I apologize, even though we'd agreed I would pull out. Still, it felt disrespectful. Disappointing.

Unnatural.

Fate wants us to mate.

That's the thought that flits through my head, and this time the idea goes beyond just marking Sadie as mine. It goes to our future. To living together. Making pups. Raising a family. Everything Sadie said she wanted, I crave to give her. I want it, too. The whole package.

"You're bleeding," Sadie exclaims, bringing her thumb to my chin.

I hurriedly swipe the evidence away. "Sorry, I—"

She studies me, concern and curiosity glinting in her warm brown eyes. "What are you sorry for?"

I swallow. I should explain it all to her. But is she ready? Are we there yet? I haven't even talked to Rafe. I don't know what I'll do if my alpha stands in the way of me claiming Sadie.

"Wolves, uh...we mark our mates."

"What?" She doesn't sound shocked. Only confused.

"With our teeth. That's why I've been going for so many

runs and not sleeping in the same bed as you. I, ah, have the urge to claim you."

"Claim me?" Her eyes are wide. Not frightened, though. That's good.

I scrub a hand over my face then pick up her yoga pants from the ground and hold them open for her to step back into. "It may not work," I admit the sour truth.

She draws in a gasp. "Do you mean, like, *turn* me?"

A surprised chuckle pops out of my throat. "No. We're not vampires." I can't stop smiling. She's so damn cute. "We're a different species. We usually mate our own kind."

Her disappointment is palpable. My wolf wants to howl, to fix it. He wants to make her happy for the rest of our lives. So do I.

I tug her back onto my lap. "I want you for my mate." I need to make it clear.

She touches my face. "I want that, too. I mean, I think I do. I want you, Deke."

"Then we'll work this out. We'll figure it out, together. All right?"

Her smile is brighter than the morning sun. She presses her lips over mine. "I love you."

"Fuck, Sadie. I love you, too."

I detect the sound of voices coming up the trail. Scott may have returned after his supreme show of cowardice to "rescue" Sadie.

"Someone's coming, Sadie-girl."

She kisses me again. "I don't care."

"I'm naked."

"Oh!" She laughs and scrambles off me.

"I'll meet you back at the resort in twenty. Okay? Are you all right on your own?"

She lets out a soft scoff. "Of course."

Of course. She was the one prepared to fight off a giant wolf with nothing but a branch. My Sadie can handle herself.

I shift, my wolf preening when Sadie gasps and buries her fingers in my fur. I risk another moment to let her stroke my ears and rub my head, then I bound up the mountain in the direction of my clothes.

When I reach the top, I turn and look down at Sadie, unable to keep my back to her for long.

She's still standing there, watching me with a wondrous expression on her face. She waves, and I lift my snout. But Scott and two resort employees are rounding the bend, so I take off, getting out of site as quickly as I can.

CHAPTER 14

adie

"WELL, THAT WAS FUN," I say as the resort grows smaller in the Mercedes rear view window. "Sex in the forest. Guess I can cross that off my bucket list. Sex with a werewolf, too."

Deke's eyes crinkle, but—characteristically—he says nothing.

After he met me back at the resort, we stayed and had another round of epic sex in the room, skipping the farewell wedding lunch.

I called for a late check-out, and we showered together then had a very late lunch before packing our bags and checking out. As much as the resort and the crowds aren't his scene, I got the feeling Deke didn't want to leave.

Like, maybe he doesn't want to get back to the real world yet. Maybe he's worried about us.

Something suddenly occurs to me. "So the *no mixing with civilians* thing, was that really, *no mixing with... humans*?"

He hesitates. "Yes and no. The thing about me being dangerous, Sadie." He looks over and my stomach cinches up. "It's real."

"We already talked that through," I say stubbornly.

"Yes, but what you didn't understand when we talked it through is that I have a wild animal inside me. And sometimes, I lose control of him."

I suddenly want to cry. Not for myself but for him. His pain is palpable.

"You didn't lose control this morning. I mean, you tackled Scott, but you didn't hurt him. You definitely wouldn't have hurt me."

He seems to consider this. His shoulders relax a bit. "Yeah. You're right. I think my fear over hurting you kept me in control."

"So you're safe. I *know* you're safe."

I do. I know it to my bones. There's no other man—werewolf—on the planet more safe for me.

As we come down a mountain and back into cell service range, my phone wakes up. It chirps at me, announcing a missed call and voicemail.

"Is that Scott?" Deke growls low. His hands instantly white-knuckle the steering wheel. It had taken me a while to shake off Scott after he so gallantly—(not)—came to my rescue with resort security. Deke showed up, though, and showed a touch of menace when he told Scott to stay away from me, or there would be trouble.

"No. My dad." I click off my phone, ignoring my missed messages. He's probably calling to see if Scott and I got back together.

It's evening when we pull up to my townhouse. It feels later than it is. The sky is dark and heavy with clouds. Deke parks, and I climb out of his ride. Before I can ask, Deke grabs my suitcase and walks me to my door. He sets my bag inside but remains outside. His big hand grips the doorframe, and he leans closer like he wants to come in but needs permission.

"I should get back to headquarters."

I don't want to pressure him, but I suddenly have this irrational fear that once he gets back to his own kind, they'll talk him out of being with me.

"Can you just spend the night tonight? Go back tomorrow?"

He scrubs a hand over his face. "I want to, baby."

"Please?" I might be doing puppy-eyes.

"Fuck, you're hard to say *no* to."

I smile.

He follows me inside.

Okay, you got him inside. Now what? "Wine?" I offer, in an attempt at hospitality.

Deke shakes his head.

Since I'm already in the kitchen, I head to the outlet I use as a charging station. I plug in my phone, and it turns on, buzzing like an angry hornet.

"Ugh," I growl when I see who's been calling me. "It's not Scott," I say to Deke, who's lurking in my living room, a giant, gloomy shadow. "Hang on." I hold up a finger, and I call my father back. It goes straight to his voicemail.

I hold Deke's gaze as I leave a message. "Hello, Dad? I'm not in the mood to talk to you. Not today and probably not for a while. Scott and I are broken up. He's a creep, and we're done. And if you don't stop trying to control me, I'm done with you too." And I hang up.

"Fuck him," I mutter and toss my phone back on the kitchen counter.

Deke blows out a breath that sounds like a laugh.

"Did you like that?" I approach him slowly, like he's a wild animal ready to run.

"Yeah." Up close, his eyes twinkle.

"I should've set boundaries years ago," I say. Step by step, I get closer. "I just needed help." When I'm close enough to touch Deke. He hasn't moved. His hands are by his sides.

"You help me, Deke. You make me brave."

"You don't need me. You're brave all on your own. You were going to rescue Scott from a wild wolf this morning."

I laugh, remembering. I still can't believe he's a wolf. I mean, I can—it seems exactly right—but it's all so fantastical.

"Well, that wild wolf likes me," I say, batting my lashes.

His eyes crinkle again.

"What about your friends? Are you worried they won't accept me?"

He hesitates, tension returning to his shoulders.

I take his hand and tug him toward the bedroom. "We can figure this out," I whisper. He follows, scooping me into the air as I cross the threshold and carrying me to the bed.

"Yeah. We'll figure it out."

Deke

I SOMEHOW MANAGE to go slow with Sadie. I guess the fact that I've already had her three times in the last twenty-four hours has soothed my wolf enough that he stays under control. I climb over my beautiful female and undress her, kissing down her neck, between her breasts, to her belly button. I avoid the most erotic zones, saving them for after the build-up. With my tongue, I trace a circle around her belly button. Then I skip to her inner thigh, flicking my tongue in a path toward home, but not touching her where I know she needs it most.

She shivers and trembles beneath me, croaking my name in those hoarse, beautiful sounds.

I take mercy and brush my thumbs over her nipples, listening to her sweet gasps, loving the way her thighs clamp together. I take one puckered bud into my mouth and suck it, hard. She arches off the bed.

"You're so beautiful, Sadie," I murmur. She should hear it. Often.

"Where would you bite me?" she asks. Like she's been thinking about it.

I freeze. "Ah, well… normally a claiming bite is here." I bring my lips to the place where her neck meets her shoulder. I kiss her there, drag my open mouth over her soft skin.

"But on a human, that could be dangerous. Shifters heal instantly, so a she-wolf doesn't mind being marked."

"Ohhh," Sadie says, eyes wide. "Can you do it… some other place? Somewhere safer?"

My heart raps quick and steady against my ribs.

Sadie wants me to mark her.

She wants to be claimed.

Do it now! My wolf roars to life, no longer content to wait.

I rear back from her, my vision sharpening as the wolf comes to the fore.

Her fingertips trace lightly over my forearms. "It's okay," she murmurs softly. I'll bet she can comfort her students in seconds with that voice. "You're in control," she tells me.

She pushes at my chest, trying to sit up. I instantly climb

off her, thinking she wants space, but she pushes me to my back. "Let me take care of you, Deke," she purrs, straddling my legs and unbuttoning my jeans.

I fist the bedcovers beside my legs as she frees my erection and runs that wet, velvety tongue around the head of my cock.

I growl, low in my throat, a growl of pleasure. So much pleasure.

Sadie licks me from balls to the tip of my cock, then flicks her tongue only over the tip a few times.

I shudder and shake beneath her, transformed by the utter satisfaction of having my female's mouth on my cock. "Sadie," I rasp. My voice doesn't sound like my own. It's deep and rough. Desperate.

She holds my gaze and slowly takes my full length into her mouth, as far as it will go before it hits the back of her throat. She uses her fist at the base to make up the difference, and starts sliding her fist and mouth up and down over my cock.

I jerk, my thighs already trembling. It feels so incredible.

"Sadie, Sadie, Sadie," I chant, losing all brain cells. "Sadie."

She hums her agreement, sending a vibration straight down my shaft to my balls. They draw up tight in reaction.

"Sadie, my sweet little human. Perfect, beautiful, wonderful Sadie."

She smiles, momentarily breaking the suction, then resumes at a faster pace. I want it to go on forever, but I won't last another minute.

I lock my knees, flexing my ankles back. My fingers wrap up tight in the bedcovers.

"I'm going to come," I warn her.

She doesn't stop, she just keeps sucking hard enough to kill me with bliss.

"Fuck!" I come in her mouth, and she goes still, then swallows and smiles.

"Oh fuck, Sadie. You are the most incredible woman on the planet."

She smiles wider.

I flip her onto her back. "My turn."

I have big plans to make Sadie scream until she's hoarse before we both fall asleep.

Deke

Darkness and humidity cover me, a warm wet cloth over my face. Suffocation, slow death, the scent of decay. I'm in a shack, bound with silver chains that burn my shifter skin. Outside is the jungle.

It's a dream. Just a dream. I fight to the surface, clawing my way out of sleep. Sinister laughter leaks into my dream, drowning out sounds of the jungle.

I jerk awake. I'm in Sadie's bed, her scent surrounding me. Her small form is beside me. But there's someone else here. Something's moving in her closet, and it's sniggers echo around the room.

"Don't you want to play?" a mocking voice cackles.

I shift and leap, ready for the kill.

CHAPTER 15

adie

I'M half asleep when the creepy laughter fills my dreams. Deke jerks awake next to me, launching out of bed.

I half sit up. "What?"

The canned laughter sounds again.

A terrifying growl shakes my walls, and I realize what's happening.

"No! Deke!" I shout. Too late. The black wolf flies at my closet, his nails scraping down the wood. It rises on hindlegs to tear open the door. Snarls fill the air.

"Deke!"

Oh crap! He thinks someone's lurking inside, and he's trying to protect me.

I get out of bed, intent on stopping him, but the snarls are too frightening. I remember Deke's warnings, his fear of hurting me. I'd be stupid to get between him and the perceived danger right now.

A crashing sound echoes off my walls as the wolf fights my closet doors and wins. Then an awful chuffing sound—the sound of a wolf devouring a stuffed toy.

"Deke."

Adrenaline flashes through me. I reach over and flip on the lights just in time to see the wolf toss the torn jackalope up into the air. It finishes it off with a snap. When he turns his great head my way, he looks like a rabid animal—no sign of humanity burns at all in that glowing green gaze.

"Oh. My. God," I whisper. My whole body shakes. Torn bits of fluff and fake fur float in the air, coat the floor, my bed, the walls.

One of my closet doors hangs askew on its hinges. The other is in pieces on the floor. My color-organized cardigans are half off their hangers.

It took Deke the wolf thirty seconds to commit this act of destruction.

I press a hand over my left breast, willing my heart to sink back into my chest.

The thing about me being dangerous, Sadie—it's real.

I DIDN'T BELIEVE him when he told me before, but I believe it now. There's a predator in my bedroom, and if for some reason it turns on me, I wouldn't stand a chance. I wouldn't survive.

"Deke," I whisper. "Come back to me."

A growl rises from the black shape in the corner. The wolf backs away, tossing its head like it's trying to jostle something loose. Then a long, low whine. The pained sound makes my heart clench. The man inside realized what he'd done.

There's a groan, and Deke rises, back in man form.

"Fuck," he says, casting a horrified glance around the room. "Sadie."

I'm pressed back against the headboard so hard, my spine's fused with it. I'm trembling so hard my muscles hurt. His feral growls still echo in my ears.

"Did I hurt you?"

He takes a step towards me, and I flinch. He sees and flinches himself.

"It's okay," I say quickly.

"No. No, it's not. I could've killed you," he says. "Fuck. Fuck!" the last time comes out a roar. I can't help my whimper.

He looks down at the wreckage strewn over the floor then back at me. "I'm sorry, Sadie." His voice cracks. "Now you see. I can't do this," he mutters. "I'm not safe."

I can't bring myself to leave the bed, but I can keep my voice steady. "Deke, look at me."

He does, and a small inhuman whine escapes him, sounding like a dog who's been kicked. Or a wolf.

I lower my hands from my heart and my mouth. I'm safe. I was just scared. My heartbeat is already slowing.

"Deke. No. Deke...it's okay—"

He turns and leaves. I scramble off my bed, grabbing a blanket to toss around my shoulders. "Wait!"

My front door slams open. I run out of my bedroom, but I'm too late.

"Deke," I cry. The neighbor's dog next door is going crazy, but there's no sign of Deke.

His car is still in front of my place, parked at the curb. No Deke. I run down my front path. "Deke!"

A giant black wolf runs down my street, leaping my neighbor's decorative fence and skidding crazily over the lawn. The last I see of its dark shape is the fanned tail and pointed ears heading into the hills.

~

Deke

I COULD'VE FUCKING KILLED her. My paws beat over the ground in a constant rhythm. I run until they're bloody, leaving wet tracks on the red earth until my shifter healing kicks in. The stinging stops for a little while, but another mile, and the rocks on the trail slice through my paws, and I bleed again.

This is the end. This is what I deserve—to run to the ends of the earth. Would that the world were flat, so I could leap over the edge. I will run until I die or until I can think of a better punishment.

Dawn breaks, and I pause in my quest. I'm on a mountain peak, surrounded by red boulders. The air is thin enough to make me lightheaded. I throw back my head, savoring the haziness in my mind. A sort of drunkenness, separating me from the pain. When clarity comes, I remember: I can never go back to Sadie.

My wolf howls and howls and howls until there's no other sound in the world.

~

Sadie

. . .

DAWN COMES AND SHEDS A THIN, sad light on the wreckage of my bedroom. I clean it up the best I can, just for something to do. I'm a kindergarten teacher, I'm used to cleaning up messes. At least this one doesn't involve peanut butter or scissors in the hands of a six year old.

But I'll never forget the savage rage, the growl in the darkness.

He's a werewolf. This was never going to work.

The closet doors aren't salvageable, so they go outside into the trash. My shredded cardigans, same. All that's left of the damn jackalope is mostly bits of black fabric and cotton fluff. I vacuum and then get dressed to go to school. Not ideal, but I have no idea what else to do. I don't know where to look for Deke. The desert? The pound? The other option is to sit in my apartment and cry.

Not an option. But I do get a little sniffly when I walk outside. Deke's Mercedes is still parked at my curb. Inside my house are his keys and his phone, all his stuff. If he comes back for it, he won't be able to get it unless I'm here.

He will come back for it, right? I hope so, but a part of me is terrified he won't. A part of me fears he's gone for good.

Deke

I RUN UNTIL NIGHT FALLS, and then I run some more.

I'm loping down the side of a mountain when a giant black wolf with amber orange markings stalks across my path. My alpha.

I skid on my aching paws. Rafe lowers his head, sniffing

me. I stay still on stiff limbs. I didn't eat today. My wolf made me drink, but I'm weak. My body trembles.

A second and third wolf rise from the brush and flank me. I'm surrounded. If I want to continue my quest, I'll have to fight it out, and in my weakened state, I'll lose.

I don't want to fight. I lower my head. Lances presses forward and licks at my side, cleaning away blood from a wound I got from tearing against a rock. On my right side, Channing presses his shoulder against mine, bracing me.

My wolf relaxes in the presence of the pack. These are my brothers, for better or worse. They heard my call, and they came.

We point our noses to the moon and howl. They sing for a brother found, but I cry for what I've lost.

Sadie

Two days pass with no sign or word from Deke. I finally cave and phone a friend. Not all of them, just Adele. I can't take a full Inquisition.

As soon as I open my door for her, Adele knows something is wrong.

"What happened?" she asks.

I press my lips together to keep the tears back, and she pulls me into a hug. "Sadie, I'm so sorry."

"I'm okay," I sniffle.

"No, you're not." Adele pulls back and studies me. "That asshole. I will end him."

"No, don't do that."

"Tell me everything."

So I do. I leave out the part about Deke being a werewolf, but I tell her everything else. The trip, the flirting, the wedding. The sex—of course I skim over those details. "We were all over each other," I summarize, my cheeks hot.

"Hmm," Adele murmurs, swirling her wine. Totally non-judgemental. "And he was a total gentleman?"

"Yes. I mean, he's intense." I blush red as Adele's wine. "Especially in bed. But I liked that. Things were fine. He told me about his past, his arrest, and we talked about it. He has PTSD from his service to our country. Sometimes it triggers violence. I was willing to work through it with him." Crap, now I have to tell her the worst of it.

"But then he…"

"He what?"

"It was the toy. The stupid jackalope. It's been malfunctioning, and it went off in the middle of the night, and Deke...went crazy."

Adele goes still. I swallow. "He didn't hurt me. But he….he thought it was a threat. He wrecked my closet. And destroyed the toy before I could stop him."

"Well." Adele sits back in her seat.

"So that was early Monday," I finish. "When he realized what he'd done, he was devastated. He told me he's too dangerous, and he took off. I haven't seen him since. I did leave a voicemail at his office." There was no answer. I spent last night by the window, waiting, wondering who else to call. "It's been two days. I'm worried."

Adele rubs her forehead, an unusual gesture for her normally poised self. She looks tired tonight, the shadows dark as bruises under her eyes. "This is a lot."

"I know." I bite my lip, desperate to defend Deke. But I need a cool head to weigh in on things. My instincts when it comes to men are all messed up.

"You care about him." The statement is more a question.

"I do. He's...he makes me strong. He never tells me what to do. Never tries to control me." Not like Scott and my dad. "He gives me space to be who I am. He likes who I am." I search for words to articulate who Deke is to me. It's impossible. A few days, and Deke has changed my whole life. "I feel stronger with him. But this violence in him… I know he won't hurt me, but my instincts might be screwed up."

"He has PTSD—it's common in vets."

"Yeah."

"Can he talk to anyone about it?"

I shrug.

Adele's voice hardens. "He needs to talk about it. He needs to do something to fix this. He's dangerous. His first instincts should be to keep you safe."

"I think they are. That's why he destroyed the toy."

"But you could've been hurt. He's willing to fight others on your behalf. But will he fight his own demons?"

Outside, a truck with a big engine rumbles past my house. If Deke's ride wasn't parked outside my house, I'd run out to see if it was him.

But then there's a knock on the door.

"Miss Diaz?" A deep voice calls. I head towards the door, peeking out the window as I do. It's Rafe. A khaki-colored Humvee idles in the cul-de-sac, Lance behind the wheel.

Adele rips the door open before I can get to it. "What do you want?" she says in a frosty tone that would cow lesser men.

Rafe doesn't cower. He does stand up straighter, like he's in the presence of a commanding officer. "I'm here to pick up Deke's ride."

"Is he all right?" I quaver.

"He'll be okay, Sadie. We found him, brought him home."

I go and grab Deke's keys, but instead of returning them to Rafe I grip them tight. "I want to see him."

"I know you do," Rafe says patiently. "But it's not a good idea."

"I just want to know that he's okay." My voice catches. Adele puts a steadying hand on my back.

Rafe angles his head to the side, a very wolf-like movement. His eyes glitter strangely in the low light. "Deke can't be with you."

Adele takes a breath, and I know she's gearing up to protest, to defend me. Rafe holds up a hand, stalling her.

"It's not you, Sadie. He can't be with anyone. He's not relationship material." He holds out his hand for Deke's keys. I relinquish them, shoulders slumping as I do. My eyes burn with tears. The clink of metal is so final. *It's really over.*

"I'm sorry, Sadie," Rafe says softly, more gently than I'd believe he could sound. "It's better this way."

"Goodbye," Adele snaps and shuts the door in his face. I wait, crying as silently as I can, until the rumbling from both vehicle's engines recedes before falling into her arms.

CHAPTER 16

"You know this is fucking jacked, right?" my brother demands.

"Excuse me?" I keep my face blank but toss the wrench I'm working with into the tool box. It's been a week since I retrieved Deke's Mercedes, but he hasn't touched it, which isn't like him. Normally this SUV is his baby. Lance and I changed the oil to see if we could tempt Deke back to normal, but no luck.

We haven't had any missions to distract us. After we got made on the last one, Colonel Johnson put the recon on Gabriel Dieter on hold. We still haven't figured out how he knew we were there.

Lance wipes his hands on the grease rag. "Something's wrong with Deke. He's fucked up. Way more than usual."

Understatement. Since we retrieved Deke, he hasn't eaten, has barely slept. Most of the time he's in wolf form.

I shrug. I can't disagree. "I'm doing all I can."

"Bullshit." Lance's cheeks are bright. He holds my eyes bravely, but his swallow belies the innate difficulty of standing up to his alpha like this. "I thought like you. I acted on orders, I went to break Deke and Sadie up. But this isn't some one-night stand. This woman's really good for him."

"Deke's unstable. His wolf can't be around humans long term. It's not safe."

"I've never seen him smile like he does with her. And he was after her from the first whiff of her scent he got. She's obviously his mate."

That stops me short. "His mate," I repeat, testing the words. *Mate.* I never thought we'd get mates. It just didn't cross my mind. "Deke has a mate."

"Yep." Lance sounds casual, but his shoulders relax. He got his message through.

Deke has a mate. Unbelievable. But my wolf confirms it's true.

"Fuck," I mutter. Keeping him from his mate will actually drive him straight to moon madness. He could be dead before the next moon. But what can we do? He can't have a human. None of us can, but especially not Deke. He's the most feral of all of us.

"This changes everything," Lance says.

"No, it doesn't. Brother. Think. Sadie's a human. Even if Deke is bound to her, we can't ask her to be shackled to him. He's a monster."

Lance is shaking his head. "He won't hurt her."

"You don't know that—"

A roar cuts me off. I kick the toolbox in my haste to race outside. Lance follows at my back. On the lawn in front of our lodge, there's a blur of white and brown, followed by a dark streak. Channing in wolf form, getting the shit kicked out of him by Deke's midnight black wolf.

"Aww hell," Lance says and starts stripping off his shirt. He sets his Rolex aside carefully before shucking off his khakis and striding, bare-assed, into the fray. He shifts, and his grey wolf joins the fight.

I sigh. Pack fights are fine, but Deke's been picking fights nonstop for days. Right now, his black wolf is growling and snapping, ripping at Channing before rounding on Lance. Channing darts away, half his ear chewed off. He looks like he wants nothing more than to slink off, but he waits patiently on the sidelines for Lance to tire, so he can run at Deke again. The only way to get Deke to stop is to tire him out. Unless we want to escalate things.

I've stayed out of the fights. If Deke turns on me, my wolf will take it as a challenge. And a challenge is a fight to the death.

Across the lawn, Lance leads Deke on a merry chase. The grey wolf's mouth hangs open, half laughing as it threads between our cars. Lance emerges from behind my Humvee, slowing to a trot. Deke is nowhere to be seen. But then—

"Look out," I shout.

Lance turns just in time for the black wolf to sail over my Humvee and crash into him. The two wolves become a blur of speed and snarls and fur. Then a pained yelp, and I wince. Deke has Lance by the nose, his fangs sunk into his muzzle. A dangerous move, and an effective one. If Deke hangs on too long, Lance won't be able to breathe.

Channing's wolf flashes by me. He hits Deke's flank and bites the black wolf's rump. Deke's head flies up, his body jackknifing in an attempt to reach Channing. Channing plants his paws and hangs on.

Lance backs away looking dazed, his muzzle bleeding.

Deke drags Channing now, trying to run in a circle to catch the brown and white wolf's tail.

This is ridiculous. Time to escalate things.

I stride onto the lawn just as Channing lets go of Deke and leaps out of the way. Deke doesn't quit. The black wolf lunges for Channing again and again.

"Enough," I order. I put the force of my alpha command into my tone. It should stop the fighting at once.

But instead of stopping, the black wolf turns and races my way, its jaw spread in a snarl as it launches at me in attack.

Deke

I GET CLOSE ENOUGH to see the whites of my alpha's eyes before Rafe throws himself out of the way. I crash into the side of the lodge, cracking a shutter. The impact makes a section of the gutter fall but the stone wall holds. I'm on my paws as quick as I land, shaking my head to clear it.

I'm broken, bleeding, but there's no way I can stop. I have to fight. There's a roaring in my ear, a sick churning in my gut. An engine fed by pain that drives me on and on.

I lost Sadie. There's nothing left for me. But I can still fight.

I'm disoriented, and by the time I get my wits back, a black and orange wolf slams into my side. I snarl and lunge, trying to catch him, but Rafe dances out of the way. He backs onto the lawn, facing me in challenge. A smarter wolf would stop and go to its belly before its alpha.

My wolf isn't smart. It wants to die. I show my teeth in a

deadly smile, and hurl myself at Rafe. This time he's ready for me, and doesn't bother skipping out of the way. He side steps and slams his shoulder into mine, unbalancing me. I find my paws again and lunge. Rafe knocks me over again. A third time, and he snaps at my haunch, a tiny nip that draws blood. And my wolf goes crazy, attacking and charging Rafe over and over as he rips into me. He's a second faster, a hair stronger, and a million times as lethal. My wolf rises to the occasion, but Rafe bleeds me little by little. And then, finally, he knocks me to my back. I try to move, and he pins me with his weight.

There are teeth on my throat. I go still.

The light is breaking in the east. My last dawn. I don't fear death. I don't welcome it either, but if I can't live with Sadie, there's no more reason for me to walk the earth.

Rafe growls against me. He's got me pinned. I scrabble my paws, hoping he'll make it quick.

"Stop," Lance is yelling. "It's a trick."

Rafe growls again but doesn't move.

"It's a trick," Lance insists. "Look at him." He points to me. "Think about how he's acting. He wants the bite."

Rafe's body goes still. And all my hopes are destroyed as he pulls away. I flip onto all fours, and I bare my teeth in Lance's direction, but he ignores me. He's figured it out.

Rafe shifts and stands as a man. "What the fuck are you talking about?"

Lance gestures to me. "He wants the bite. He's trying to get you to kill him. Whenever he had you in a hold, he didn't kill you. He kept going until you had him pinned. He's not out of control. He planned this."

"Is this true? Suicide by Alpha?" Rafe crouches to look me in the eye. I duck my head. "If that's true, then you are in control, more than you think." He grips the scruff of my neck and hauls my head up again. I show him my fangs, but I don't mean it. Fight's over.

"Change," Rafe orders, and my spine bows backwards as the wolf releases my body.

Rafe backs away, giving me space. In man form, I'm still bleeding, but my wounds are healing.

"Bastard," I mutter, but I take my alpha's hand when he offers to help me up. He grips my shoulder, and I wince. My skin is still sensitive from the shift.

"This changes everything," Rafe says.

"No," I growl, but inside my heart, my wolf raises his head, wanting so desperately to believe.

Sadie

It's my father's phone call that changes everything. It's Wednesday, a school night, and I'm pacing in my living room. I cancelled our girl's night. I can't eat, can't sleep, can't think. I had a few days with Deke, a few days of heaven, and now I'm left with nothing. My ovaries are in bed, eating bon bons and moping. My heart is a cracked and bleeding mess.

My phone buzzes. I snatch it up and answer on autopilot.

"Sadie," my father's nasal voice drones. "Finally. I've been wondering if you were still alive."

The sarcasm barely registers. "Yeah."

"That last voicemail was something else." He pauses, and I don't say anything. If he's waiting for me to apologize, he will have to wait the rest of his life.

My father clears his throat. "Now that I have you on the phone, I want to talk to you about Scott. I think—"

Oh my God! Will this man never listen?

"I only dated him for you," I interrupt with sudden, blazing clarity.

"Excuse me?" My father sounds affronted, but I don't care. If anything, it's a bonus.

"I only dated him for you," I repeat. "You were nicer to me when I was with Scott." It's true. All the barbs, the little digs, the insults—they stopped when I was with Scott. I used Scott as a shield between me and my dad just for some relief. Except Scott was worse.

"You both treated me badly." I can't believe I didn't see it before.

"Listen—"

"No, you listen. You don't get to treat me like I'm a child or someone lesser. Those days are done. I don't need Scott. And I don't need you." I hang up.

Already I feel lighter. My instincts aren't wrong. I just never listened to them before. It's time I stop listening to other people. They don't know what's best for me. They might think they do, and they might have some good advice, but my life is my own. My choices.

And my happiness is available, right in front of me. I just have to reach out and take it. No one's going to hand it to me, and it doesn't matter. I can choose happiness for myself.

That's how I find myself in my car, coaxing my little Hyundai up the mountain road. The little engine is slow to propel me forward, but slowly we gain elevation. And then I'm turning into the road for the lodge and speeding down that thickly wooded way. I pull into the parking lot in front of the garage big as an airplane hangar. Deke's black Mercedes

G63 is there, and so is his bike. My heart squeezes and thumps.

Here goes nothing.

~

Deke

"IT CHANGES NOTHING," I rasp at my alpha. But he keeps grinning at me.

"You're in control, Deke," he says. "You always have been."

I step back, away from Rafe, and glance at Lance, at Channing. Both my packmates are nodding.

"But what does this mean?" I know what I hope for, but it's too good to be true.

Rafe must know I'm reeling because his voice is gentle. "It means you have a mate."

A mate. I run a hand over my head, trying to catch my breath.

The sound of an engine makes my eyes snap up, alert. A little white Hyundai rolls down our drive and up to our garage. I only know one person who drives a car like that. My legs weaken, and I'd fall to my knees if I wasn't so wounded and my wolf wasn't so adamant that I not show weakness right now.

Sadie's here.

~

SADIE

I get out of my car and startle when I realize Deke's right there on the lawn, a few feet away from my car.

"Sadie?" Deke calls. He's naked with blood marring his skin.

He's all ripped up. Has he been fighting? Behind him Rafe and Lance are tugging on their jeans. I see blood on them, too, and they all look shameful. I've broken up quite a few scraps on the playground, and I know those guilty looks.

There's a huge brown and white wolf behind them, lurking on the edge of the woods. Channing? Geez, these werewolves are big.

"Who did this to him?" I demand in my best teacher voice. I glare at his friends who all grow more sheepish. My legs tremble, but I hold my ground.

Deke makes a sound low in his throat and steps between his alpha and my line of sight. I refocus on him.

"Deke. Have you been fighting?"

"What are you doing here?" His voice is rough, like it hurts him to talk. I take a step towards him. I want to soothe all his wounds. "I'm here for you. For us."

He tilts his head in that wolfish way of his. I can't read his expression.

"You can't get rid of me so easily." I fist my hands at my sides. "We had something good together. You think you're dangerous to me, but I know you're not. You would never hurt me. You won't." I shake my head for emphasis.

Deke's packmates slink back, giving us some space.

"Deke, I want this. I want you. And I'm going to figure out what it takes to have you. We don't have to go too fast. We can take it slow and—oof!"

In two strides Deke has me up in his arms. I throw mine around his shoulders and hang on. Behind us, Rafe and the rest of his pack are grinning. Rafe nods, and Lance winks and gives me a thumbs up. Then Deke and I are in a garage.

"Where are you taking me?" I ask. My heart beats fast, adrenaline at war with anticipation. Normally I'd think it's rude for a guy to scoop me off my feet and carry me off wherever he wants, but with Deke I'm happy to be along for the ride. "I don't mind. I'm just curious."

"My room. My bed. Now."

He carries me up a flight of stairs and into a cavernous room with rough wooden beams crisscrossing a cathedral ceiling. There's a California king sized bed right under the huge windows. It's covered with a big white comforter, and the room is surprisingly neat. Or not so surprising, considering this is Deke, and he's careful with his things.

Deke sets me down on the floor next to the bed.

Then he's kneeling and gripping my middle. My shirt has ridden up, and his face presses into my belly.

"I'm sorry," he says, his words muffled against my skin. "I'm sorry." *My sweet savage werewolf.*

"Deke," I stroke his head. "There's nothing for you to be sorry about. You had a bad episode. It happens—to humans, too. We can work through it."

He huffs out a sigh and squeezes me tighter.

"It's okay." I slide my hand along his jaw, lifting his face to mine. "I'm here now. I'm not going anywhere."

The bunched muscles in his shoulders lift and fall as he sighs. Deke rises, lifting me at the same time. He lays me down on the big bed, and I sink into the fluffy white comforter.

"I want you to know how much you mean to me." He moves over me, pining my wrists in a dominant yet somehow gentle move. "I need you to know." He kisses down my neck and licks the same spot over and over. Then he turns his head to the side and groans.

"Is everything okay?" I ask.

"I need to mark you, Sadie. If you're really sure you want me."

"I want you," I promise.

"You have to be sure. Once I mark you, I'll never let you go."

"Mark me." I've never been so sure about anything in my life.

His big body shudders over me. "Fuck," he rasps. "How did I get so lucky?" And then he's kissing me again, pulling up my shirt so that he can scrape his teeth along my breasts. Given what he just told me, I'm nervous but that doesn't stop my body from succumbing to pleasure.

He works his way down, kissing my belly, peeling off my jeans and rubbing his full face against my pussy. He pulls aside my panties and licks me, pinning my thighs down with his big hands, so I can't snap them together. Not that I want to. My hips are rising, grinding, offering up my lady parts to his tongue. His rough stubble scrapes deliciously over my smooth skin, sending pleasure-pain signals sizzling to my brain. My neurons short circuit, catch fire, shoot sparks. My werewolf is eating me in the best way.

My what a big tongue you have…

I come with a howl and jackknife in half, folding over Deke's head. He growls, sending a fresh wave of adrenaline tingling to my fingertips. He unwraps a condom and rolls it on. Then his big body rears over me, his cock nudging its blunt head between my tender folds. I'm super wet for him, but I hiss as he stretches me and arch again as he bottoms out so deep inside me I can taste him.

"Yes, yes, yes," I chant as his hips rock forward. The slow drag of his cock in and out lights up the pleasure center of my brain. But the real magic comes when his giant rod batters the back of my womb, hitting some crazy arousal spot. Deke's deeper inside me than anyone's ever been, and it's ringing my bell. *Ding, ding, ding, you win an orgasm!* Carnival lights flash behind my eyes. I can only lie beneath him, body shuddering with each constant wave of climax, as he saws in and out of me. Each thrust bangs the headboard against the wall. I thought this bed looked sturdy, but I shouldn't have underestimated the intensity of a werewolf screw. Deke works over me, every muscle in his chest standing out in relief as he bares his teeth and fucks me deep. Fire dances in his dark emerald eyes.

"Mine," he growls. His hand slides up my chest until his fingers collar my throat. "Only mine."

Yes! I want to shout, but my mouth is lax. The constant stream of orgasms is destroying me.

In my haze, I see Deke's mouth yawning open in a roar. His teeth are whiter and longer than ever, the canines sharp and elongated. Time spirals slower, and everything in me clenches in anticipation of his bite.

Deke roots himself deep, groaning. His fangs graze the top of my shoulder. I sense him shaking, and I realize it's from the effort of holding back.

"Do it," I whisper. The dangerous scrap of his teeth awakens something primal in me. I reach up and grasp the back of his neck. "Yes."

But the muscles of his neck are taut under my palm. He tosses his head back and forth, fighting himself.

"Do it. Do it now," I whisper. He keeps thrusting, the force of his movement making the headboard beat against the wall in a booming rhythm. I dig my nails into his shoulders, marking him. "Do it!"

Deke rears back, his canines glinting and then snaps his head forward, sinking his fangs deep into my shoulder. Pain and pleasure slice through me, the sensations swelling and filling me with light and heat and flashes of fire.

"Yes," I pant against the deep ache in my shoulder. "Yes."

Deke withdraws, and the pain in my protesting muscle dissolves, sending white hot streaks of lightning sizzling to my core.

This is it. This is forever.

CHAPTER 17

adie

THE WIND BLOWS my hair as I stand outside, overseeing recess on the playground. I have gauze over the puncture wounds, but they're healing quickly. Deke dotes over me like crazy, trying to give me ibuprofen and cleaning the wounds with the healing properties on his tongue every chance he can get.

Still, I can tell he loves the mark, as well. His gaze goes soft every time he looks at it. He trails kisses all along my neck and across my collarbone and tells me how much he loves me. How he's going to take care of me and protect me for the rest of our lives.

He also says marking me has calmed his wolf significantly. He doesn't need to go out and run all night anymore. He's content to stay at my place and protect me from any savage toys in my closet.

"Miss Sadie, look," Owen cries and points. There's a big moving truck backing into a parking spot right beside the playground.

I wave to the teacher assistant, so she'll know to watch my half of the class, and head to the fence to see what's going on. Several of my students have already gathered there.

"Army men," Jackson announces. My breath catches as Deke jumps out of the passenger side of the cab followed by Rafe on the driver's side. The alpha gives me a wink and heads to the back of the truck. Deke strides straight for me.

"What is this?" I ask when he gets close.

"Delivery for you," he says then looks at the kids pressing their faces against the fence. "For all of you."

Behind him, Rafe opens the truck door. Out jump Lance and Channing. Inside the truck are stacks and stacks of black boxes.

"Jackalopes," Jackson and Owen scream in unison. The werewolf pack makes a chain, tossing a steady stream of black boxes down the line.

"Is this okay?" Deke waits for my nod before he starts handing the boxes to each kid.

"You bought one for everyone in the class?" I ask when I find my voice.

"For everyone in the school," Rafe calls.

"Batteries included," Channing adds.

"Great," my teacher assistant mutters. She's surrounded by a sea of kids holding their creepy, red-eyed toys, trying to administer order among chaos. It's creepy as hell, but I can't move, can't speak.

"You okay?" Deke asks softly. The rest of the pack have moved on, probably to find the principal and figure out a way to deliver the world's most coveted toy to every kid in my school.

I'm all choked up. In the past few days, I've learned so much about Deke, about his service, his nightmares. His life as a shifter. I even got to talk to a lion shifter couple, Nash and Denali. Nash served in the military, and Deke has been in contact with him daily, opening up about his PTSD.

But my favorite conversation was with Amber Green, a human woman who's mated to a werewolf alpha in Tucson. She had a lot of advice for dating a werewolf and made me promise I'd call her whenever I needed to vent. "It's hard, but it's worth it."

And looking at Deke, I know what she means. Here he is, watching me with his dark eyes, a little guarded, a little worried, trying so hard to make things right.

I love him more than ever. A little jolt goes through me. *I love Deke Adalwulf.*

Well, duh, my ovaries roll their eyes.

"Sadie?"

All my kids are distracted by their toys, so I slip out of the playground and approach my werewolf.

"I can't believe you did this." I let out a watery laugh. "How did you do this?"

He shrugs. "Figured it was the least I could do, since I destroyed the classroom toy."

A cold wind blows, and I step closer to him. Shifters run hotter than humans, I'm discovering. Especially when they're around their mates.

Sure enough, I step close, and Deke's heat and scent surround me. He reaches out and pulls up my coat collar, shielding me from the wind.

"I'm going to get better," he promises.

"I know."

"I'm going to do it for you." He presses his forehead against mine.

"I know," I whisper. I rise to kiss him. Even on tiptoe, I only reach his chin. He dips his head and hauls me up with a hard arm around my waist. I melt against him, kissing him properly before pulling back my head to whisper, "Darling, think of the children."

He growls but lets me down. My class didn't notice our PDA, each kid too absorbed with their own personal Jackalope.

I'm about to ask him how exactly he found all these toys when Deke's head snaps up. His nostrils flare, and he grimaces like he's scenting something rotten.

"Sadie," a harsh voice calls. I look up and see my father stalking out of the school. Automatically, I step closer to Deke.

"What's going on here?" My father surveys my class with distaste twisting his mouth. Inside the playground fence, Jackson chases a little girl with his toy. Both kids scream with delight. I'm going to have to buy headache medicine for all my teacher friends and their assistants.

But it's worth it.

"Sadie," my dad shouts again. I know I should go and introduce Deke as my boyfriend. But I'm so tired of trying to get his approval, and I already know it won't come where Deke is concerned. I suddenly see my dad for what he is: a bald, pot-bellied white man with an over-inflated sense of authority.

I turn back to Deke. "You know what, fudge it," I say and surge back into his arms. Judging by his harrumph, my father gets the message, and I am left to lose myself in my mate's kiss.

~

Sadie

"And that's how Deke won the love of every kid in the school," Charlie finishes, her bottle of Fat Tire beer raised in the air.

"My goodness, this is a long toast," Tabitha mutters.

Charlie flicks her middle finger up, tilting her bottle of beer and nearly spilling the liquid.

"A toast to Sadie and Deke," Adele says smoothly, raising her own wine glass and stopping the fight before it begins.

I sip my wine and smile. It's Whine Wednesday, and we're at a new restaurant outside of town, not far from Deke and the pack's HQ. Nestled in the mountains, it's a rustic chophouse with a huge fireplace and giant, cozy leather chairs. One taste of the parmesan truffle fries, and we unanimously voted to come here at least once a month.

"So what did your dad say when he met Deke?" Charlie asks, stuffing a fry in her mouth.

"He didn't say anything," I respond. "I didn't introduce them. He's not currently part of my life."

"That's good. Make him grovel." Tabitha nods approvingly.

"He doesn't need to grovel. He just needs to respect me and my choices. And if he doesn't, well, I'm not going to waste any more time on him."

"Here, here," Tabitha and Charlie cheer, raising their beers.

"I'll drink to that," says a deep voice behind me. I turn even though my skin is tingling, already alerting me a predator is near. *My* predator.

Deke stands beside our table, gazing down at me. He

must have been in Werewolf Stealth Mode. I didn't even hear him approach.

"Deke," I say and fly out of the seat into his arms. He lifts me for a kiss that leaves me breathless. The room's spinning a little when he sets me down. He hugs me to him, and I hang on like I've had too much whiskey.

"What are you doing here?" Adele snipes, and I realize that three huge shadows have coalesced out of the back of the restaurant—the whole pack is here.

"We're here to celebrate Whine Wednesday," Lance says, dragging a chair over and dropping into it right next to Adele. She looks down on her nose at him which is funny because she's a head shorter.

"We own this place," says Rafe, copying his brother and seating himself at Adele's right.

"We need a chef, actually," Rafe leans back in his wooden chair and looks right at Adele. "Someone who knows how to run a business."

I go still. Adele's been telling us of her troubles running the chocolate shop. Her business partner is acting strangely, disappearing for weeks and taking personal loans from their business bank accounts without warning and vague promises to "pay the business back." Last week, Adele had to pay the shop's rent out of her own savings.

She's even taking private catering jobs to make ends meet. This job might be a godsend. My eyes dart between the two of them: Adele posh and pretty in her vintage dress—Rafe casual and dangerous in his fatigue pants and a faded green Army t-shirt that makes love to each of his abs. The pack alpha balances on the back two chair legs, somehow managing to look relaxed even as his muscles are taut.

"I'll let you know if I think of someone," Adele says coolly.

Rafe holds her gaze a moment then lifts his chin. He murmurs in his deep voice, "You do that."

Adele sniffs and turns her back to the Alpha.

"We were just toasting Sadie," Tabitha explains to Lance and Channing. Lance keeps shooting looks at Charlie, but she seems to be ignoring him. Which is interesting.

"Why?" Channing asks. "Is she preggers already?" He raises his eyebrows and pretends to inspect my stomach.

Adele chokes on her wine.

"No," I answer. "You goof." I know Channing's just joking, but the thought of a baby with Deke makes me so happy. My ovaries are ready. I snuggle closer to Deke, who squeezes my shoulders. "We were celebrating me finally growing a backbone and standing up to my father."

"You always had a backbone. Your dad and Scott just never respected it," Adele says.

A growl rumbles in Deke's chest at the mention of Scott's name. I lay a hand on his pec.

"Yeah, whatever happened to Scott?" Charlie asks.

Tabitha shrugs. "He's gone. Last I heard, he moved to Florida. Probably to put up beachfront condos."

"Good riddance," Adele mutters.

"Let's get out of here," Deke murmurs to me. His tongue touches the edge of my ear, followed by a tiny nip of his teeth. I jump.

"Deke and I are just going to...uh...get some air," I say and steer him to the door to the large deck outside.

"You kids have fun," Tabitha calls.

Behind me, I hear Adele growl under her breath, "If he isn't good to her, I swear they will never find his body."

"I'll vouch for him," Rafe's voice rumbles in reply. I turn to see Adele narrow her eyes at Rafe before I duck outside with Deke.

"What's going on between those two?" I ask Deke as we head to the deck railing. Above the sky is midnight blue, the Milky Way spilling starlight in a glistening veil over the dark shapes of the mountains.

"Which two?" Deke asks.

I frown, rubbing my hands together in the cold. "Adele and Rafe. Who did you think?" The sight of Charlie carefully ignoring Lance flashes through my head.

"No one," Deke answers so blandly I know he's noticed something between Charlie and Lance too. "But Adele came to the lodge and confronted Rafe. She told him if he didn't get me and the rest of the guys into therapy, she would personally slit our throats."

"Oh." That sounds like Adele, actually. Momma bear. "I didn't tell her about… you know." The werewolf thing. "Your secret's safe with me."

"I know, baby. I don't think you'll have to keep it a secret from her much longer."

"Really?"

"Really." He pops my collar, tucking it tighter around my face before wrapping me in his arms, his heat. "Rafe's been sniffing around Adele. And not just because something's up with her business."

My forehead creases. I want to ask what's going on with her business, but it's really none of mine. I make a mental note to ask Adele myself. "Do you think she's his mate?"

"Don't know. Rafe doesn't think he deserves a mate. None of us did. You were unexpected. A gift."

"Deke," I whisper. My heart is so full right now, it's as big as the moon, spilling its light over the world.

Deke lifts me onto the railing, holding me close as he dips his head near to mine. "I'll have to warn him about the worst thing about dating a human."

"What's that?" My head is swimming with his scent.

"Shapewear," he says against my mouth, and I giggle as we kiss and keep each other warm under the frosty sky.

EPILOGUE

adie

No one gives head like a werewolf. My throat is hoarse from screaming when I roll over to answer my buzzing phone. My mate keeps me more satisfied than I could have ever imagined. He put a ring on my finger, too. Even though the mating bite is all that matters to wolves, he understands that humans have their own traditions. I told him it didn't matter to me, but Deke insisted I get everything I dreamed of.

He reaches past me to snatch up my phone, immediately alert.

"It's Charlie." He hands it to me.

"Hello?" I rasp, swallowing a few times.

"Sadie?"

I climb out of bed. "Charlie—how have you been, girl? I haven't seen you around."

"I've been...busy. But—"

"Are you crying?"

"What? No. Of course not."

"You don't sound okay."

"Yeah, I need to talk," Charlie chokes.

"Okay."

"I have a teeny tiny problem. You know Deke's friend—the hot blond one?"

"You mean Lance?" I wrinkle my nose. I suppose Lance is hot, but I don't think of him that way.

"The one who looks like he could front a boy band," Charlie says drily.

"He's a bit more buff than that."

"Okay, then, a *Baywatch* remake."

"I'll give you that. Lance does have a surfer-dude vibe going on. What about him?"

"We might have hooked up."

"Oh. Oh my. You and him?"

"Yeah. I know. It was on a whim."

"Good for you. I mean, it was good right?"

"Better than good."

"I'm glad. So what's the problem?"

Charlie heaves a sigh, which sounds like a gale wind over the phone. "It was supposed to be a one-time thing."

"Okay."

"Even though we really were great together."

"Okay…"

"And now I have a problem." She pauses, and I bite my tongue before I demand her to just spit it out.

"I'm pregnant."

~

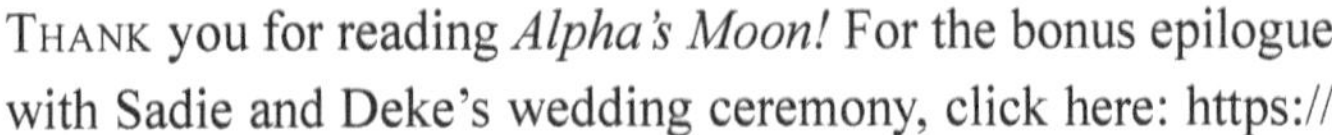

THANK you for reading *Alpha's Moon!* For the bonus epilogue with Sadie and Deke's wedding ceremony, click here: https://

BookHip.com/MPMAPDL. If you enjoyed the book, we would so appreciate your review, as they make a huge difference for indie authors. Be sure to sign up for Renee and Lee's newsletters for news about the release of ***Alpha's Vow*** and ***Alpha's Revenge***!

WANT FREE BOOKS?

Go to http://subscribepage.com/alphastemp to sign up for Renee Rose's newsletter and receive a free books. In addition to the free stories, you will also get special pricing, exclusive previews and news of new releases.

Download a free Lee Savino book from www.leesavino.com

OTHER TITLES BY RENEE ROSE

Paranormal

Bad Boy Alphas Series

Alpha's Temptation

Alpha's Danger

Alpha's Prize

Alpha's Challenge

Alpha's Obsession

Alpha's Desire

Alpha's War

Alpha's Mission

Alpha's Bane

Alpha's Secret

Alpha's Prey

Alpha's Sun

Shifter Ops

Alpha's Moon

Alpha's Vow

Alpha's Revenge

Wolf Ranch Series

Rough

Wild

Feral

Savage

Fierce

Ruthless

Untamed

Wolf Ridge High Series

Alpha Bully

Alpha Knight

Midnight Doms

Alpha's Blood

His Captive Mortal

Alpha Doms Series

The Alpha's Hunger

The Alpha's Promise

The Alpha's Punishment

Other Paranormal

The Winter Storm: An Ever After Chronicle

Contemporary

Chicago Bratva

"Prelude" in Black Light: Roulette War

The Director

The Fixer

"Owned" in Black Light: Roulette Rematch

The Enforcer

Vegas Underground Mafia Romance

King of Diamonds

Mafia Daddy

Jack of Spades

Ace of Hearts

Joker's Wild

His Queen of Clubs

Dead Man's Hand

Wild Card

Daddy Rules Series

Fire Daddy

Hollywood Daddy

Stepbrother Daddy

Master Me Series

Her Royal Master

Her Russian Master

Her Marine Master

Yes, Doctor

Double Doms Series

Theirs to Punish

Theirs to Protect

Holiday Feel-Good

Scoring with Santa

Saved

Other Contemporary

Black Light: Valentine Roulette

Black Light: Roulette Redux

Black Light: Celebrity Roulette

Black Light: Roulette War

Black Light: Roulette Rematch

Punishing Portia (written as Darling Adams)

The Professor's Girl

Safe in his Arms

Sci-Fi

Zandian Masters Series

His Human Slave

His Human Prisoner

Training His Human

His Human Rebel

His Human Vessel

His Mate and Master

Zandian Pet

Their Zandian Mate

His Human Possession

Zandian Brides

Night of the Zandians

Bought by the Zandians

Mastered by the Zandians

Zandian Lights

Kept by the Zandian

Claimed by the Zandian

Stolen by the Zandian

Other Sci-Fi

The Hand of Vengeance

Her Alien Masters

Regency

The Darlington Incident

Humbled

The Reddington Scandal

The Westerfield Affair

Pleasing the Colonel

Western

His Little Lapis

The Devil of Whiskey Row

The Outlaw's Bride

Medieval

Mercenary

Medieval Discipline

Lords and Ladies

The Knight's Prisoner

Betrothed

The Knight's Seduction

The Conquered Brides (5 book box set)

Held for Ransom (out of print)

Renaissance

Renaissance Discipline

ALSO BY LEE SAVINO

Paranormal romance

The Berserker Saga and Berserker Brides (menage werewolves)

These fierce warriors will stop at nothing to claim their mates.

Draekons (Dragons in Exile) with Lili Zander (menage alien dragons)

Crashed spaceship. Prison planet. Two big, hulking, bronzed aliens who turn into dragons. The best part? The dragons insist I'm their mate.

Bad Boy Alphas with Renee Rose (bad boy werewolves)

Never ever date a werewolf.

Tsenturion Masters with Golden Angel

Who knew my e-reader was a portal to another galaxy? Now I'm stuck with a fierce alien commander who wants to claim me as his own.

Contemporary Romance

Royal Bad Boy

I'm not falling in love with my arrogant, annoying, sex god boss. Nope. No way.

Royally Fake Fiancé

The Duke of New Arcadia has an image problem only a fiancé can fix. And I'm the lucky lady he's chosen to play Cinderella.

Beauty & The Lumberjacks

After this logging season, I'm giving up sex. For…reasons.

Her Marine Daddy

My hot Marine hero wants me to call him daddy…

Her Dueling Daddies

Two daddies are better than one.

Innocence: dark mafia romance with Stasia Black

I'm the king of the criminal underworld. I always get what I want. And she is my obsession.

Beauty's Beast: a dark romance with Stasia Black

Years ago, Daphne's father stole from me. Now it's time for her to pay her family's debt…with her body.

ABOUT RENEE ROSE

USA TODAY BESTSELLING AUTHOR RENEE ROSE loves a dominant, dirty-talking alpha hero! She's sold over a million copies of steamy romance with varying levels of kink. Her books have been featured in USA Today's *Happily Ever After* and *Popsugar*. Named Eroticon USA's Next Top Erotic Author in 2013, she has also won *Spunky and Sassy's* Favorite Sci-Fi and Anthology author, *The Romance Reviews* Best Historical Romance, and *has* hit the *USA Today* list seven times with her Wolf Ranch series and various anthologies.

Please follow her on:

Bookbub | Goodreads

Renee loves to connect with readers!

www.reneeroseromance.com

reneeroseauthor@gmail.com

ABOUT LEE SAVINO

Lee Savino is a USA today bestselling author, mom and chocoholic.

Warning: Do not read her Berserker series, or you will be addicted to the huge, dominant warriors who will stop at nothing to claim their mates.

I repeat: Do. Not. Read. The Berserker Saga. Particularly not the thrilling excerpt below.

Download a free book from www.leesavino.com (don't read that either. Too much hot, sexy lovin').

www.ingramcontent.com/pod-product-compliance
Lightning Source LLC
Chambersburg PA
CBHW030334310726
48979CB00001B/20
9781636931135